"_____ myself
a_____ _____ered._"

"You'd better tell me now," Allie urged.

Before Lorne could speak, his security man said in awed tones, "I have the honor to present His Royal Highness, Prince Lorne de Marigny, ruler of the sovereign islands of Carramer."

She felt faint, but this time it had less to do with the pounding she had taken in the surf than with the impact of the man standing before her. "You're the ruler of the whole country?"

Lorne nodded.

The combined effect of her ordeal and the discovery that she had been rescued by the monarch himself combined to overwhelm her precarious hold on consciousness. The security man's startled cry and Lorne's barked command were the last things she heard before she saw the sand rushing up toward her.

THE CARRAMER CROWN

The Monarch's Son—available now
The Prince's Bride-To-Be—available next month
The Princess's Proposal—available late September

Dear Reader,

Looking for sensational summer reads? All year we've been celebrating Silhouette's 20th Anniversary with special titles, and this month's selections are just the warm, romantic tales you've been seeking!

Bestselling author Stella Bagwell continues the newest Romance promotion, AN OLDER MAN. *Falling for Grace* hadn't been his intention, particularly when his younger, *pregnant* neighbor was carrying his nephew's baby! Judy Christenberry's THE CIRCLE K SISTERS miniseries comes back to Romance this month, when sister Melissa enlists the temporary services of *The Borrowed Groom*. Moyra Tarling's *Denim & Diamond* pairs a rough-hewn single dad with the expectant woman he'd once desired beyond reason...but let get away.

Valerie Parv unveils her romantic royalty series THE CARRAMER CROWN. When a woman literally washes ashore at the feet of the prince, she becomes companion to *The Monarch's Son*...but will she ever become the monarch's wife? Julianna Morris's BRIDAL FEVER! persists when *Jodie's Mail-Order Man* discovers her heart's desire: the *brother* of her mail-order groom! And Martha Shields's *Lassoed!* is the perfect Opposites Attract story this summer. The sparks between a rough-and-tumble rodeo champ and the refined beauty sent to photograph him jump off every page!

In future months, look for STORKVILLE, USA, our newest continuity series. And don't miss the charming miniseries THE CHANDLERS REQUEST... from *New York Times* bestselling author Kasey Michaels.

Happy reading!

Mary-Theresa Hussey

Mary-Theresa Hussey
Senior Editor

Please address questions and book requests to:
Silhouette Reader Service
U.S.: 3010 Walden Ave., P.O. Box 1325, Buffalo, NY 14269
Canadian: P.O. Box 609, Fort Erie, Ont. L2A 5X3

The Monarch's Son

VALERIE PARV

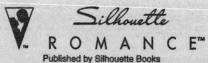

ROMANCE™

Published by Silhouette Books

America's Publisher of Contemporary Romance

To my darling Paul,
the real prince in my life

SILHOUETTE BOOKS

ISBN 0-373-19459-5

THE MONARCH'S SON

Copyright © 2000 by Valerie Parv

This edition published by arrangement with Harlequin Books S.A.

Visit Silhouette at www.eHarlequin.com

Printed in U.S.A.

Books by Valerie Parv

Silhouette Romance

The Leopard Tree #507
The Billionaire's Baby Chase #1270
Baby Wishes and Bachelor Kisses #1313
*The Monarch's Son #1459

**The Carramer Crown

VALERIE PARV

lives and breathes romance, and has even written a guide to being romantic, crediting her cartoonist husband of nearly thirty years as her inspiration. As a former buffalo and crocodile hunter in Australia's Northern Territory, he's ready-made hero material, she says.

When not writing about her novels and nonfiction books, or speaking about romance on Australian radio and television, Valerie enjoys dollhouses, being a *Star Trek* fan and playing with food (in cooking, that is). Valerie agrees with actor Nichelle Nichols, who said, "The difference between fantasy and fact is that fantasy simply hasn't happened yet."

HISTORY OF CARRAMER

The Carramer Crown takes place in the fictitious island kingdom of Carramer in the South Pacific. French explorer la Perouse called Carramer "the loveliest fleet of islands anchored in any ocean." Carramer comprises three inhabited islands and a handful of tiny offshore islands. The main island is Celeste, home to the capital city of Solano, and the ruling monarch, Lorne de Marigny. Across the Carramer Strait lies the larger, blissfully beautiful Isle des Anges (Island of the Angels) and its near neighbor, tiny Nuee, both governed by Prince Lorne's younger brother, Michel, next in line to the throne after Lorne's son, Nori. Younger sister Adrienne sees no role for herself in government, and yearns to establish a horse-breeding stable.

Carramer's traditions are a mixture of French and Polynesian influences. It enjoys a perfect climate, as near-constant trade winds prevail throughout the year and most rain falls as daytime showers that are accompanied by rainbows, giving rise to the popular name for Carramer of "the Rainbow Isles."

There is rumored to be another royal offspring living in the United States, but so far that story remains untold.

Valerie Parv
Official historian to the sovereign state of Carramer

Chapter One

As soon as Allie Carter felt the powerful undertow start to drag her out to deep water she knew she was in trouble. The current flowed as fast as a river, much too powerful for her to swim against. It was all she could do to keep her head above water.

Every instinct urged her to fight her way back to the fast-receding beach, but she resisted the temptation, knowing it was the way to certain death. Instead she made herself swim parallel with the shore. She knew that sooner or later the current would dissipate in calm water, then she could turn toward land, although judging by the ferocity of the current, it was likely to be a long way from Saphir Beach where she'd entered the water.

"Let it take you, don't fight it," she told herself to curb her rising panic. She couldn't help thinking about the sharks that frequented the deeper waters. Maybe they only ate women from Carramer and not visiting Australians, she thought. Talk about wishful thinking. The thought distracted her briefly from the growing ache in her shoulders and arms, although it did nothing for the rawness of her throat from swallowing salt water.

Just when she was afraid she wouldn't have the strength to make it back to shore, she felt the current's grip slacken, and she began angling her strokes to carry her to a cove visible in the distance. Exhaustion and salt water blurred her vision but she thought she saw someone moving about on the sand, unless it was more wishful thinking.

By the time she reached shallower water she couldn't summon the energy to stand up, and she flopped in the breakers, chest heaving with the struggle to breathe, barely able to see out of stinging eyes. Waves washed over her head and threatened to carry her out to sea again but she had no strength left to fight them.

Suddenly she felt herself being lifted into strong arms and carried the last few feet up the beach. "It's all right, you're safe." The French-accented voice sounded powerfully male, although the man himself was an infuriating blur. With an odd sense of detachment she felt herself being placed on her stomach on an unyielding surface. A heavy pressure made itself felt on her back and she tried to protest but couldn't force the sound out. The pressure returned several times at steady intervals until she coughed, bringing up copious amounts of seawater.

"Much better," the vibrant male voice commented as if to himself, adding to her, "lie still while I get a doctor."

Groggily she rolled over onto one elbow and struggled to focus on her rescuer. *Looming* seemed like a good word to describe the tall, broad man bending over her. But his voice sounded concerned, and the hands that placed a folded towel under her head and offered her another to clean her face were gentle. When he leaned over her, she was enveloped in a tantalizingly elusive scent, something expensive and French and very, very masculine.

"I don't need a doctor. I'll be fine if I can rest for a few minutes," she croaked, hoping she sounded more convincing to him than she did to herself.

"You are far from fine. You almost drowned in the grip of the serpent." This time he sounded definitely disapproving.

She felt spent but knew she wasn't delirious. "The serpent?"

"Local folklore. You Australians would call it a rip. An undertow. You obviously haven't been in Carramer very long or you would know that Saphir Beach is dangerous unless you know these waters well."

Her temper wasn't helped by her exhaustion and the awareness of how close she'd come to drowning. She didn't need this stranger to point out that it was due to her own stupidity and lack of local knowledge. "I wasn't to know, was I?" she snapped. "The only warning signs were in Carramer language."

"How surprising."

The sarcasm in the man's voice wasn't lost on her. She struggled to sit up and found herself lying on thick woven matting under a white canopy that reminded her of a sheik's tent. She blinked hard, realizing uncomfortably that she must have washed up on one of the many private beaches around the island kingdom. Its owner, as his behavior suggested he was, sounded annoyed by the intrusion.

Her vision had nearly cleared, and almost against her will she was intrigued by the man meeting her curious gaze. In spite of his disapproving expression he had the most arresting features she had ever seen, strongly carved as if from stone. Only the working of a muscle at his jawline belied this impression.

His obsidian eyes glared at her from under hair of almost the same color. Gold flecks glittered in the dark pools of his gaze. Something familiar about him tugged at her, although she was so tired she could barely think straight.

Another question occurred to her. "How did you know I'm Australian?"

He frowned, censure in every line of his face. "If your accent hadn't betrayed you, your beauty and your boldness would have done so."

She seized on his last points. "Are you telling me that Australian women have a *look* you can recognize?"

He nodded. "Your particular robustness is quite different from the delicacy of Carramer women, even when you're as slender and shapely as you are, Miss…"

He tailed off, clearly expecting her to supply a name. "Alison Carter," she said, pleased to hear her voice sounding less husky already. "Allie to my friends."

"Alison." The curt way he said her name immediately removed him from the friend category. "I am Lorne de Marigny."

"Pleased to meet you, Monsieur de Marigny." She matched his formal tone and granted him the locally preferred French appellation almost unconsciously. In Australia she would have called him Lorne without a second thought, but his upright bearing and stern manner suggested that it wouldn't be wise, for some reason. Oh well, when in Rome or Carramer, she thought. Summoning her limited reserve of strength, she struggled to her feet. "Thank you for your help, but I'd better go."

A wave of dizziness caught her and she swayed. Instantly his arm came around her shoulder, supporting her. "You are in no condition to go anywhere until you have been cleared by a doctor."

His supportive arm felt so good that she was tempted to lean into his embrace and let him continue making decisions for her. He sounded accustomed to it, and she was very, very tired, but she couldn't impose on him any longer when he clearly resented her presence. "No, thanks.

You've done more than enough. I'm sorry I intruded on your privacy, but I'll leave now.''

The black gaze bored into her, his closeness emphasizing the intensity in his expression. ''Precisely how do you plan on leaving?''

She hadn't thought that far ahead. ''I guess I'll walk back to Allora. I'm staying at a hostel there.''

He dismissed the notion with a curt gesture. ''In the first place, you're in no condition to walk anywhere, far less a couple of miles back to the town.''

She started in surprise. ''The current took me that far?''

''It has been known to.'' He sounded dryly amused.

She could hardly wait for the second place. ''And?''

''You're seeing a doctor before you go anywhere. Come, my villa is over the rise.''

He clearly took her compliance for granted, and she lifted her head in automatic defiance. ''Next thing you'll tell me you keep a doctor on call.''

Lorne merely looked at her. ''As it happens I do.''

''And a chauffeur and a helicopter complete with pilot, too, I suppose?''

He inclined his head slightly. ''Among other staff, yes.''

She couldn't restrain her outrush of breath, feeling more like a fish out of water than ever. A nearly drowned fish at that. Either this prepossessing stranger had delusions of grandeur or he was a man of some importance. She squared her shoulders. No matter who Lorne de Marigny was, where she came from, one person was as good as another. ''I don't see any staff around here right now,'' she said with a pointed glance around them.

His black look impaled her. ''Are you questioning my word?''

He sounded as if it was a rare event. Maybe it was time somebody did. ''In Australia we call things as we see them," she stated, her gesture encompassing the empty beach.

He dragged in a deep breath and she could practically feel him restraining his temper. "Make no mistake, we are under observation from several quarters even now. This beach is well known to be off-limits to the public, and my staff is trained to be discreet, giving me at least the illusion of privacy."

Unlike certain foreigners, came the unspoken criticism. "Look, I didn't plan on washing up on your private beach," she protested, tiring of his imperious attitude and his insulting suggestion that she required watching. What harm could one bikini-clad tourist possibly do to a man of his impressive physique? "If one of your...staff...will give me a lift back to Allora, I'll get out of your hair. I promise I'll see a doctor as soon as I get back," she added before Lorne could say any more on the subject.

His dark brows drew together. "Are you always so annoyingly persistent?"

"Only when half-drowned," she assured him tiredly. Her every muscle ached from fighting the current, and her legs weren't doing too well at holding her up. She was in no state to deal with Mr. Arrogance even if it turned out that he owned half of Carramer.

He regarded her in obvious disbelief. "Why do I doubt that it takes a bout with the serpent to bring out this tendency in you?"

On the other hand he had saved her life, she conceded to herself. "When I was four, my mother called me Miss One-Note because she said I was so single-minded," she confessed, not entirely sure why. "I guess I haven't changed."

"I imagine you have changed considerably since you were four," he commented, appraising her so frankly that she was left in no doubt as to the changes he was referring to.

His blatantly masculine scrutiny reminded her of how much her white bikini revealed. Having forgotten to pack her own swimsuit, she had purchased the bikini locally yesterday, allowing the saleswoman's enthusiasm to override Allie's misgivings about its brevity. She hadn't allowed for the way the twin bands of stretch material molded themselves to her body when wet, revealing even more of her shapely figure than they had when dry.

Well, so what if they did, she told herself defiantly. It wasn't as if she had anything to be ashamed of. She was no supermodel, but a careful diet and exercise routine had given her curves in all the right places. All the same, Lorne's slow inspection provoked a tingling sensation in the pit of her stomach that had nothing to do with nearly drowning. It came to her that she felt more out of her depth beside Lorne on the sand than she had in the grip of the undertow.

"You'd better take the lead," she suggested in an unsteady voice.

He inclined his head, his expression darkly amused. "I invariably do."

As he took her arm and steered her toward a narrow path skirting a dune, the heat of his hand seared her skin as if a naked flame had touched it. She glanced in surprise at the strong fingers cupping her elbow. No flames, only ordinary flesh and blood. Her exhausted state must be the reason why his touch sent shivers dancing along her spine. Maybe he was right and she would be wise to consult a doctor after all.

"What brings you to Carramer? Are you on vacation?" he asked as she tried vainly to match his long-legged strides. He noticed and moderated them a little.

His disinterested tone suggested that he was only making

polite conversation. "It's a working holiday," she supplied. "I came here to paint."

"You are an artist?"

Again she caught the disapproval in his tone and wondered at its source. Her sigh was more betraying than she intended. "That's what I want to find out. Back home in Brisbane I teach art at a girl's school, but I've always wanted to paint professionally. I decided to spend some accumulated leave exploring what I can achieve."

"Why Carramer specifically? Surely you can paint in Australia?"

She nodded. "I could, but there are too many distractions."

His eyebrow lifted. "Distractions as in a man?"

Distractions as in a family for whom she had always been on call, she thought, automatically suppressing a flash of resentment. Between a constantly ailing mother who expected Allie to parent *her*, and a spoiled younger sister who thought her needs should always come first, there had never been much time or money for anything Allie herself wanted.

Her father had left them when Allie was sixteen, and since then her mother had looked to her daughter for support, swearing that she couldn't manage alone. Her many ailments could never be specifically diagnosed but prevented her from working full-time and ensured that Allie was always there for her, doing all she could to make her mother's life easier. She had even abandoned her dream of attending art school in favor of teacher training so she could bring in enough money to help put her sister through university.

Then a few months ago, Alison's mother had dropped the bombshell that she intended to marry a neighbor who had apparently courted her while Alison was at work. Nothing was said in words but it was made clear that it was time Alison made a life for herself. She was duly thanked for all she had done but shown clearly that her sacrifice was no longer necessary.

Lorne mistook her silence for agreement. "Was this man cheating on you?"

Alison's confused gaze flew to his face. "No, I mean there is no man. I came for my own reasons."

He looked skeptical. "You're telling me that a woman of your obvious charms has no man waiting for her at home?"

She would have taken it as a compliment if not for the painful knowledge that Lorne was right. Supporting her family and dealing with their emotional demands left her little room for a love life. She'd dated a colleague from school but he was, if possible, more demanding than her family, even objecting to this vacation because she wouldn't be at his beck and call.

Suggesting that he might not wait for her return was intended to bring her to heel. She wasn't sure who had been more surprised when she agreed that it was probably better that way. "There's no man waiting at home anymore," she denied, unable to keep an edge of bitterness out of her voice.

"I suppose your own needs took priority." Lorne's cutting tone was a judgment in itself.

At his high-handed tone resentment surged through her. She had had enough of ordering her life around the demands of people who were only too ready to shrug her off when it suited them. Now it was time for some changes. Unconsciously she lifted her chin. "What's wrong with pleasing myself?"

He paused before replying. "In my experience, it usually means riding roughshod over the feelings of others."

It was the last thing she would do, but she was too drained by her near drowning to feel like defending herself to Lorne. What would he know about the price her responsibilities had exacted from her, anyway? From his extraordinary good looks and talk of his villa and staff, it sounded as if he didn't have anyone but himself to worry about.

She shot him a sidelong glance, confused by her ambivalent response to him. His take-charge attitude should have bothered her, but instead it excited her at some unexpected level. She forced herself to ignore the fluttering in her stomach and study him as he had studied her. He was indeed as tall as she'd first concluded, but not dauntingly so, perhaps a head taller than Allie herself. His straight back and easy carriage created an intriguing impression of leashed power.

His hawklike features should have been alarming but instead she found herself imagining how he would look in a moment of joy, the dark eyes lightening with pleasure and the full-lipped mouth curving into a smile. A shiver ran through her.

She would like to paint him exactly as he looked now, she thought. Wearing sleek black swim briefs that rode low around narrow hips, he nevertheless managed to look aristocratic, like a knight in full regalia. Trying to capture that quality would challenge any artist. He looked as if he knew exactly where he fitted into the world.

She suppressed a surge of envy. It must be wonderful knowing exactly who you were and what you should be doing, something Allie herself was still trying to sort out. "What do you do here?" she asked on impulse.

He looked baffled for a moment then said, "Do? You could probably say I run things."

She was intrigued in spite of herself. "You mean like a manager? In business or government?"

His compelling mouth tightened. "You haven't been in Carramer very long, have you, Alison?"

"A week, but I plan to stay as long as my money lasts. Why? Should I know who you are?"

He shook his head. "No, but I suspect you're about to find out."

She followed the direction of his gaze to where a dark figure plunged toward them from the trees beyond the cove. Then she saw a man in pursuit of a much smaller figure pelting across the sand.

"Nori," Lorne said, his voice softening with such affection that she regarded him curiously. He opened his arms, and the child threw himself into them, wrapping both arms around the man's neck as if he would never let go. "What are you doing here? You're supposed to be taking a nap," Lorne asked.

"Don't need a nap, I'm a big boy now." The child's voice was a piping imitation of Lorne's vibrant French-accented voice.

For some reason Allie felt a stab of disappointment. There was no doubt that Lorne and Nori were father and son. The resemblance was far too strong. So he was married. She didn't know why it bothered her, as their paths were unlikely to cross again, but the discovery felt as uncomfortable as a grain of sand in her shoe.

The child looked from the stranger to his father. "This is Alison Carter. She got into trouble with the serpent and isn't feeling well," Lorne explained.

The little boy nodded gravely. "I know to be very careful of the serpent and only swim with my nanny."

Allie couldn't help smiling. With huge dark eyes that shone like stars and skin the color of honey, Nori looked utterly captivating. The mischief dancing in his expression only made him look more appealing. "Maybe I should only swim with my nanny, too," she agreed.

The little boy looked scornful. "You're too big to have a nanny. When I'm big, I won't have one, either."

Allie laughed. "How old are you, Nori?"

"I'm a big boy now. I'm four." He held up three chubby fingers, the little finger and thumb curling into his palm.

Without stopping to think, Allie straightened the little finger alongside Nori's extended fingers. "This many fingers make four."

The child frowned. "I know that. I was teasing."

It ran in the family, she thought. Taking the child's hand had brought her close enough to Lorne to feel the whisper of his breath against her cheek, bringing with it another trace of the masculine French aftershave lotion mingling with his own compelling male scent. The combination spoke of balmy walks under the stars and moonlit swims and endless nights in the arms of a lover. She blinked hard. The experience of nearly drowning must be affecting her more than she realized.

The moment was shattered when a solidly built man in a white shirt and dark trousers lumbered up to them. "I'm sorry about the interruption, Your Highness. Nori insisted on seeing you and took off before his nanny or I could stop him."

Shock rippled through Allie and her legs started to buckle. *Your Highness?* No wonder Lorne had expected her to recognize him. A detail she had barely absorbed from the guide book came rushing back to her: de Marigny was the name of Carramer's ruling family. She had gatecrashed the royal residence. If she hadn't been so groggy from her ordeal she would probably have recognized his name.

You take the lead. In her head she replayed her own foolish words and his imperious reply. *I usually do.* At least she hadn't called him Lorne. The penalty for that was probably beheading with a rusty sword or some such. It was a wonder he hadn't called his guards instead of coming to her aid himself when she washed up at his feet. As it was, she couldn't have made a bigger fool of herself if she'd tried.

"It seems I owe you an apology, Your Highness. I had no idea," she said, holding her anger in check with difficulty. He might have told her the truth and saved her a lot of embarrassment, but she could hardly say anything without making matters worse.

He waved away her concern. "It was a novel experience not to be recognized."

Her blood began to boil, threatening to overrule common sense. "I'm glad I provided a diversion, Your Highness. Court jesters must be in short supply in Carramer."

Her anger evidently caught him by surprise. "Contrary to what you think, I wasn't amusing myself at your expense. I had intended to introduce myself properly as soon as you were fully recovered."

"Then you'd better tell me now," she urged. "I don't want to make a bigger fool of myself than I've already managed to do."

Although she spoke softly, the security man looked startled. Evidently people didn't speak to members of the royal family like that very often. Before Lorne could speak, he said in awed tones, "I have the honor to present His Highness, Prince Lorne de Marigny, ruler of the sovereign islands of Carramer." The man sounded astonished that such a self-evident fact needed stating.

She felt faint again but this time it had less to do with the pounding she had taken in the surf than with the impact of the man standing beside her, his arms around an adorable four-year-old who must be the heir to the throne of Carramer. Her voice seemed to come from a long way off as she said, "You're the ruler of the whole country?"

Lorne nodded, his black eyes shining. "So it would seem."

The combined effect of her ordeal and the discovery that

she had been rescued by the monarch himself combined to overwhelm her precarious hold on consciousness. The security man's startled cry and Lorne's barked command to take the child from him were the last things she heard before she saw the sand rushing up toward her.

Chapter Two

As Lorne scooped up Alison's inert body, he automatically reassured his son. "It's all right, Nori. Miss Carter is only tired because of her fight with the serpent. Return to the house with Robert and I'll bring Miss Carter myself." To his aide he added quietly, "Have the doctor meet us there."

The bodyguard was too well trained to argue the prince's edict, but his eyes were full of questions as he took Nori and hurried toward the villa. Lorne knew he had always been something of a hands-on ruler, but it was unusual for him to take such a personal interest in a stranger even if she was inordinately beautiful. Of course, most strangers didn't wash up on the beach at his feet, he admitted to himself.

Alison didn't stir when he held her in his arms for the second time in an hour. Much more of this and it could get to be a habit. He frowned as he took in the paleness of her features. They were already finely drawn, and her pallor added to his impression that he held a life-size porcelain doll.

Smudges of violet rimmed her huge sea-green eyes. He felt annoyed with himself for letting her talk instead of insisting she see his doctor right away. Who knew what damage her brush with the serpent had done?

He had allowed her to talk because he had enjoyed it, he acknowledged inwardly, crossing the white sand in long strides until he reached a row of ironwood trees fringing the beach. Meeting a woman on equal terms was a rare experience in his world, where almost everyone knew who he was at first sight and invariably reacted with deference. It had come as a shock to realize that Alison had no idea of his position. Then he had started to enjoy being treated as a man rather than a monarch.

Fool, he berated himself. Hadn't he learned anything from his experience with Nori's mother? Chandra had been Australian, too, and as refreshing in her way as Alison was in hers when they met during an official visit to her country. He had fallen in love with the former Miss Australia and against the advice of his ministers, had brought Chandra back to Carramer as his bride.

The fantasy had lasted only long enough for her to realize that, unlike her reign as Miss Australia, her duties as a member of Carramer's royal family wouldn't end after a year. During one of their more spectacular arguments, she had assured Lorne that attaining the title of princess had been her ambition all along. Having achieved it, she could see no reason to put up with the duties attending the title.

Motherhood had proved even more of a burden and she had readily handed their son over to a nanny until Lorne stepped in, taking an active role as the baby's father. Chandra simply hadn't cared about either of them, preferring to fly off to Paris where she could attend the latest fashion showings and revel in the attention she received as a princess without the inconvenience of royal duties.

In desperation Lorne had reduced her allowance, forcing

her to stay at home for longer periods, only to be accused of being a tyrant with no thought for her needs and feelings. Over time, she found almost everything about the island kingdom disagreeable—including their marriage, leaving Lorne feeling more alone than he had ever felt when he was single.

Chandra also grew increasingly resentful of the attention Lorne devoted to their baby and retaliated by criticizing everything to do with Carramer. His country could never compete with Australia in her eyes. He had become sick of hearing how much better everything was in Australia. Yet he couldn't do the one thing Chandra really wanted him to do—free her from their marriage vows so she could enjoy being a princess without any other ties.

In his country marriage was a union for life. Only in the most dire of circumstances could separation be considered. There was no such thing as divorce. A couple might live apart, but they would be bound together until death. Chandra had demanded that Lorne change the laws, but having seen the effects of divorce on children in other countries, he couldn't bring himself to institute it in Carramer, not even for his wife. Had they not been royal, he could have allowed her to live apart from him, but he had no intention of setting such a poor example for his people.

A furrow etched his brow. If he had changed the law, would Chandra be alive today? He would never know. He only knew that another fierce argument had resulted in her flight away from the villa at reckless speed, ending when her car went out of control on a cliff top, sending the car crashing to the surf below. Chandra had found her release but in a way that would haunt him for the rest of his life.

The woman in his arms moaned softly, drawing his attention. While they talked, her long hair had dried into a curtain of nut-brown curls that now fanned out against his shoulder. Silken strands of it twined around his fingers. He caught himself wondering at how little she weighed, surely not much more than Nori. The feel of her lithe body against him reminded him unwillingly that it had been a year since Chandra died, a long time for a man of his strong appetites to be without the company of a woman.

The frown returned. What was it about Alison Carter that made him so aware of his celibate life? After Chandra he knew better than to involve himself with a woman not of his own kind, especially another Australian. What was their expression? Once bitten, twice shy. It definitely applied to him. And he wasn't so starved for female attention that any woman would turn his thoughts in the same direction.

There was something about *this* woman that affected him in ways he preferred not to think about, he knew. The sooner his doctor cleared her to be on her way, the better for all of them.

When Lorne reached the villa, Dr. Pascale was pacing the marble terrace, his expression anxious. As soon as he saw Lorne, he gestured for servants to relieve the prince of his burden. Lorne gave Alison up to them with a reluctance he didn't care to examine too closely.

"Take her to the Rose Suite," he instructed. Of all the guest suites in the villa, it was the most beautiful. An artist would appreciate waking up in such surroundings, he thought. To the doctor, he said, "Report to me as soon as you've examined and treated her."

The doctor's eyebrows lifted curiously. "I take it this young lady is special to you?"

The doctor had brought Lorne into the world thirty-one years ago and was one of the few people who would dare to speak so familiarly to him. Lorne's parents had died during a cyclone when he was only twenty, and the doctor had become something of a father figure. The man's informality usually warmed him, but right now he found it intensely irritating. "She is a stranger in need of our help, Alain. I suggest you provide it for her."

The doctor didn't look in the least put out by Lorne's abruptness. "As you wish, Your Highness." Somehow he managed to infuse the title with a touch of reprimand.

Lorne regretted his tone immediately. He deserved Alain's censure. No matter how confused he felt over the unexpected arrival of the Australian woman, it didn't give him the right to abuse a dear friend. Raking long fingers through his hair, Lorne said, "Wait, Alain. I'm sorry for snapping at you. Do what you can for her, all right?"

Amusement danced in the doctor's expression. "As you wish, Your Highness." This time, the title contained the wealth of affection that had built up between them through the years.

By the time the doctor returned with his report, Lorne had showered and changed into a white open-necked shirt and black pants. He was surprised at the tension he noticed coiling inside himself as he waited for the doctor's verdict.

"The young lady has suffered no lasting harm from being caught in the rip," the doctor informed him. "At least no physical harm."

Alarm flared through Lorne. "Then why did she faint?"

The doctor paced to a large window overlooking the villa's expansive grounds. "Exhaustion would be my diagnosis."

"From her ordeal?"

The doctor turned back to him and shook his head. "From more than that, I would say. She's run-down and slightly anemic. When she came around, she was groggy enough to be honest and admit she hasn't taken a holiday for years. I gather she hasn't had much sleep since arriving in our beautiful country."

Bracing himself, Lorne said, "I imagine she spends her nights partying with other travelers her own age."

"I doubt it," Dr. Pascale observed dryly. "She's staying at Shepherd Lodge."

"I see." Lorne did see. Shepherd Lodge was run by an order of lay nuns who took strict care to see that their residents behaved themselves. The young women who stayed there endured the spartan rooms and requirement to do chores either to please parents who lived in the country or, in the case of foreigners, because it was clean and incredibly cheap. He had a good idea which of the reasons applied to Alison. On the beach she had mentioned staying as long as her money lasted.

"I've given her something to help her rest," the doctor continued. "Do you want me to arrange transportation for her back to the Lodge when she wakes up?"

Lorne was in no doubt what answer the doctor expected. Alain Pascale might be getting on in years but he was nobody's fool. "You know perfectly well I can't send her back to that bleak place if she's unwell," he observed testily. "They have a rule against residents remaining in their rooms during the day. You have to be almost dying to be exempted."

"Then she can remain in the Rose Suite for a day or so until she recovers?"

Wondering if he needed his head examined, Lorne nodded. "For a day or so. Have someone notify the matron at Shepherd Lodge that their resident is staying at my villa so they have no need to send out a search party."

The doctor's eyebrows lifted. "And you got mad at me for harboring suspicions. *They'll* have nothing on the rumors doing the rounds once that message is received."

Lorne gave a heavy sigh. "You're right as usual. Have my aide tell them Alison has taken up a post with my household as…as Nori's companion for the remainder of our vacation here."

Alain had the grace not to grin, although he looked

pleased by the decision. "You're assuming that she'll accept, of course."

Lorne wondered if he looked as stunned as he felt. "Of course she will, if I command it."

The doctor shrugged. "You of all people should know Australians can be infuriatingly independent. Miss Carter seems to be no exception. I'd ask her nicely if I were you, then she might say yes."

Asking nicely wasn't something Lorne was accustomed to doing. As the sovereign ruler of Carramer, his word was quite literally law. For the first time it came to him to wonder if it hadn't been one of the stumbling blocks to happiness with his late wife. Since he would never know the answer, he dismissed it from his mind. "I'll think about it," he said ominously.

"I recognize a dismissal when I hear one," the doctor said easily. "I'll stick around overnight in case your young lady needs me again."

"She isn't my young lady," Lorne said irritably. "Although I seem to be stuck with her for the time being."

"Approach her with that attitude and it won't be a problem. She'll be gone so fast your head will spin," the doctor pointed out. "Most virile young men wouldn't consider accommodating a beautiful young woman to be a hardship."

Lorne favored him with his most regal glare of disapproval although he knew it was wasted on the doctor. "Most virile young men don't have a country to run."

"Or a bad experience with an Australian beauty behind them," the doctor observed with remarkable insight. "Remember, not all women from that country are like Chandra. Some of them enjoy living in Carramer."

Alain Pascale's wife, Helen, was one of them, the prince knew. A nicer, more generous person was impossible to meet. Even in her late sixties, she was still a beauty, and although she returned regularly to visit relatives in her native country, her loyalty to Carramer was unwavering.

"Neither are they all like Helen," Lorne countered. "She may be Australian, but her heart belongs to Carramer."

The doctor laughed. "Give me some of the credit at least. When you're as much in love as Helen and me, even after forty years of marriage, it hardly matters where you live as long as you're together."

Jealousy gripped Lorne so fiercely it was like a physical pain, but years of royal training enabled him to mask the reaction. He kept his expression impassive as he bade the doctor good evening. "You may have only one patient, but I have a million of them and I need to get some work done, vacation or no," he explained.

At the door the doctor paused. "You may have a million subjects, but you're still a man with a man's normal needs and desires. Maybe you needed to have a woman wash up at your feet to remind you of the fact. Good night."

Before Lorne could frame a scathing reply, the doctor had gone and Lorne was alone. Never before had his private apartment seemed so vast or lonely, he reflected somberly. Maybe the doctor was right. It was time he got to know one or two of the beautiful women who were regularly paraded before him at official functions. One of them would never capture his heart unless he gave them a chance. Somehow the idea had less appeal than he thought it should.

"Good, you are awake. Papa said no one was to disturb you until you woke up by your own self."

It took Allie a moment to connect the child at the foot of her bed with her surroundings, then she sat up with a jolt as memory came rushing back. She had almost drowned in the undertow known locally as the serpent and had been rescued by Prince Lorne himself. She remembered collapsing at his feet, then awakening briefly to find herself being checked over by a kindly doctor who said he would give her something to help her rest.

"What time is it?" she asked the wide-eyed little boy watching her intently.

He made a face. "I don't know, I'm only four. You went to bed even earlier than me, Miss Carter."

She couldn't help smiling and realized how much better she felt. "I did, didn't I, Nori? I'd like it if you called me Allie. It's the name my friends use, and I hope you'll be my friend, too." She levered herself onto one elbow and patted the space beside her. "Jump up."

He didn't need a second invitation. "You talk funny."

"I'm from Australia. That's why I sound funny to you."

He settled himself more comfortably beside her. "My mummy came from Australia. Is that like Heaven?"

Something was wrong here. "Australia's a place like Carramer, Nori," she explained, adding gently, "is your mummy in Heaven?"

The child nodded and his eyes grew luminous. "Papa says we can't visit her but she's very happy."

Allie's heart felt as if a giant hand had clamped around it. So Lorne's wife had been Australian, too, and had died not so long ago. She remembered the cold way Lorne de Marigny had identified her nationality. Allie must have reminded him painfully of his loss. He must have loved his wife a great deal to react so strongly, she thought on a wave of sadness. What must it be like to be so loved? "I'm sure your daddy's right, sweetheart," she assured the little boy tremulously.

He nodded, then brightened. "Do you have a pet kangaroo in Australia?"

He was so sweetly earnest that she wanted to hug him, but hesitated. Was one allowed to hug a crown prince, even if he was only four years old? She settled for placing an arm around his small shoulders. He responded by nestling into the crook of her arm, triggering a surge of maternal longing deep inside her. "No, I don't," she said with a laugh. "Kangaroos are wild animals that live in the bush, not in people's houses. But I have cuddled a koala. They're adorable, like you."

He looked disgusted. "I'm not 'dorable. But I'd like to cuddle a koala."

"They're only found in Australia and a few zoos in other places. Tell you what," she said on a sudden inspiration, "I have a toy koala in my luggage back at Allora. I promise I'll send it to you as soon as I get back there."

"There's no need. Nori has plenty of toys," came a stern injunction from the doorway.

Allie turned to see Lorne standing there, looking like thunder. It was very attractive thunder, she couldn't help thinking, as memories of him carrying her up the beach returned unbidden. He was dressed in a light-blue polo shirt with a monogram on the pocket and navy pants, the fine cut of the clothing emphasizing the athletic figure underneath. She pulled the bedclothes up higher in an instinctively defensive gesture.

At the sight of his father, little Nori scrambled off the bed and ducked under his father's arm out of the room. Lorne said something to him about a nanny waiting with breakfast, and the child scampered off.

"I would rather not have my son's head filled with fantasies about Australia," the prince said grimly.

What had she done? "I only promised him a toy koala," she explained. "I brought one with me in case I needed a gift, so it's no problem."

He folded his arms across his broad chest and angled his body against the door frame, a picture of masculine disapproval. "Perhaps not to you. But Nori already thinks of

Australia as a kind of Disneyland where everything is more exciting than in his own country.''

The child probably associated all Australians with his mother and endowed them with the same magic, Allie thought. She wondered if Lorne knew just how much the little boy missed his mother. Without knowing more of what had happened, she didn't feel free to bring it up. And she had already made enough mistakes where Lorne was concerned, starting with treating him as a commoner instead of the most powerful man in Carramer.

"About yesterday, Your Highness," she began formally, although the effect was reduced somewhat by their relative positions. "I'm sorry for intruding. Thank you for having your doctor treat me and for letting me recover here, but I should get back to Allora."

"Alain—Dr. Pascale—has prescribed several days' rest for you," the prince informed her. He didn't sound pleased about it. "He tells me you're run-down and slightly anemic."

It was said as if he found her a complete nuisance. Her temper flared. "I didn't plan on collapsing at your feet, Your Highness. I'm sure I can recuperate just as well at my hostel if you'll let me dress and be on my way."

She dimly remembered the doctor helping her to change, after having had clothing brought to her room, presumably from some royal storehouse. Turning her head, she could see several garments folded neatly over a stand under a window. One of the other teachers at the school where she worked would have called the situation "landing on her feet." Looking at the prince's forbidding expression, Allie wasn't so sure. "I'll make sure you get your clothes back safely," she added.

The prince shook his head. "The clothes are unimportant. Dr. Pascale wants you to remain here."

That made one of them, she thought tensely. She sat up,

forgetting for a moment that the doctor's bounty had included a decidedly skimpy nightdress that revealed as much of her as it covered. With difficulty she resisted the temptation to drag the covers back over herself. There were other, more important issues here. "Surely I have some say in this?" she demanded.

It was the wrong tone to use, she saw, when anger flared in the prince's black eyes, but all he said was, "If you were from Carramer, you would know better."

"Because you're the prince and I'm nobody?" she asked. He might be the ruler of his country, but he wasn't *her* ruler, and it was time she pointed it out.

If her comment amounted to high treason, he took it remarkably calmly. "Your status is irrelevant. I was referring to Dr. Pascale's prescription of rest and quiet for you."

The thought that Lorne wouldn't allow her to stay for any other reason added fuel to her annoyance. It was clear that, doctor's orders or no, the prince would like nothing better than to send her packing. She probably reminded him too painfully of the Australian wife he had lost. But Lorne wouldn't want to risk having her collapse again if he let her leave before the doctor okayed it. And in truth, she did feel shakier than she had any intention of admitting.

The prince saw it, anyway. "Rest now," he instructed. "Your accommodation has been informed that you are remaining here, and your luggage will be brought later this morning."

"You've thought of everything," she said mutinously.

He chose to ignore her tone. "Precisely. To allay any unseemly rumors, they have also been informed that you are joining my staff as a temporary companion to the crown prince."

This was interesting news, given that Lorne obviously didn't want her anywhere near his little son. "And am I?"

"Of course not. Nori seems to enjoy your company, but he is already well looked after."

He was also a lonely little boy, but she had a feeling Lorne wouldn't welcome that observation. "Then I'm afraid I can't stay," she said, pushing back the bedclothes.

It was a mistake, she realized as soon as she swung her legs over the side of the bed. The nightdress barely reached her thighs. Lorne had seen much more when he rescued her from the surf wearing only a bikini, but she hadn't felt as exposed then as she did now.

She was acutely conscious that this was a bedroom and Lorne was first and foremost a man, a man among men, she recalled him being described in her guide book. She had thought the phrase extravagant and was alarmed at how readily it sprang to her mind now. He made her feel a sense of herself as a woman that she hadn't felt in all the years that she had served as her mother's housekeeper and younger sister's caregiver.

She refused to let him see how much he discomfited her and stood her ground beside the bed, wishing that the room would stop moving around her and spoiling the effect.

"Get back into bed. You're in no condition to go anywhere," he commanded, but his voice had gentled and he moved to her side, steadying her. "Let me help you."

She could have managed to stay upright if only he hadn't touched her, but as soon as he took her arm her knees turned to jelly and she sagged against him. "I won't stay here under false pretenses," she insisted, trying to ignore the tattoo her heart had set up. It was a symptom of her weakened state, nothing more, she insisted to herself.

His deeply vibrant voice was very close to her ear. "Obviously you have yet to learn that one does not say no to royalty."

Lorne might be used to his subjects shaking in their shoes when he looked at them, but she came from stock that had made an art form of equality. Respect was another matter, but it had to be earned, and riding roughshod over her preferences was no way to earn it. "And you have yet to learn that we Australians are an independent lot who prefer being asked to being told," she said as coolly as she could manage.

His expression turned grim. "During my marriage, I was made well aware of your Australian disdain for authority, but you are in Carramer now. You will stay because the doctor advises it." He didn't add "and I command it" but he might as well have. She heard it in his steely undertone.

"Or you'll do what? Throw me over a cliff like the guidebook says your ancestors did?" Her chin came up and she almost closed her eyes as the gesture brought her face alarmingly close to his. She settled for lowering her lashes slightly so she looked at him through a feathery screen. It softened the strong contours of his face but not by much.

The glint in his gaze clearly said "don't tempt me" but the only outward sign of his anger was in the rigidity of his arm around her and the sudden tightening of his jaw as he said, "Please get back into bed."

Surprise almost knocked the wind out of her. "There, see? Saying please didn't hurt a bit, did it?"

As soon as the whispered words were out, she cursed herself. What was it about the prince that made her open her mouth and say stupid things? Lorne was a man who plainly wasn't used to deferring to anyone. What would it have cost *her* to be gracious? Instead she had to issue what amounted to a challenge.

She should have known better, she grasped, as she glimpsed the light of battle in his eyes. Then his head came down and his lips claimed hers. Like many grown women, inside Allie was a little girl who had dreamed of one day being kissed by a prince, but nothing in her childhood fantasies had prepared her for the reality. Instinct told her that

Lorne was only showing her who was boss, but the molten way he made her feel overruled logic, leaving a sensation so all-consuming that she didn't want it to end.

When he put her away from him, she was glad of the bed at her back as her knees buckled. She curled her fingers around the edge of the mattress for support. "I wasn't aware that your customs included the one about *droit du seigneur*," she said shakily.

"Supposing it was not just a medieval myth. The right of the ruler to have any woman of his choosing before any other man hasn't been claimed for centuries," he said equably. The coldness in his expression reminded her that he hadn't kissed her out of desire, but because she had challenged his authority.

"But you think it did exist?" She suppressed a shiver at the possibility.

His mouth curved into a perceptive smile, making her wish she had fought him when he kissed her. Why hadn't she? "It would be...edifying," he confirmed after a long pause, "but it has nothing to do with why I kissed you."

She tossed her head, wishing she had more energy to put into the defiant gesture. His kiss had added to her feeling of weakness in ways she was probably better off not thinking about. "I know perfectly well that you did it to show that I may have won the round but you will win the match because of who and what you are."

He inclined his head in agreement. "Then we both know where we stand."

He was only confirming what she had suspected, but part of her rejected the thought that it was his only reason for kissing her. In the midst of her own maelstrom of feelings she had sensed an equally strong response in him. Clearly he did find her attractive, but it was plain that she reminded him painfully of the Australian wife he had lost, so he was unlikely to give in to it.

It was fine with her, too, she thought. After years of burying her own needs and desires in favor of her mother's and sister's, she wasn't interested in exchanging one form of tyranny for another. Lorne was the last person in the world who should interest her romantically. He was too hard-headed and his position made him far too inflexible for there to be any common ground between them.

All the same, his kiss lingered on her lips long after he left her to sleep, and although she closed her eyes, it was a long time before her need for rest overcame the turmoil racing through her mind.

Chapter Three

The morning was well advanced by the time Lorne dismissed his aide and stood up from his desk. He stretched luxuriously, feeling his muscles unknot. He wondered briefly what it would be like to enjoy a vacation as others did, totally free of the responsibilities that even rested on his shoulders when he was at his summer residence, away from the capital. Like Alison, came the involuntary thought. No affairs of state troubled her, not even affairs of the heart, it seemed.

The state of her heart wasn't his concern, he told himself fiercely. Until the doctor cleared her to return to her hostel, she was merely another responsibility. Lorne had no need to see her unless he chose to. The villa had more than enough staff to take care of one stray Australian who had had the misfortune to wash up on their private beach. Why was he wasting time thinking about her when his son was waiting?

Alison continued to occupy his thoughts as he changed for Nori's daily swimming lesson. The task could have been delegated to the palace's personal trainers, but Lorne enjoyed teaching his son himself, and Nori looked forward to having his father to himself and showing off what he had learned.

Today, however, Nori sat on the edge of the pool looking downcast. Lorne dropped to the marble coping beside his child. "What's the matter, *coquine?*"

Nori's small chin jutted out. "I'm not a little rogue. I'm a good boy."

Lorne nodded, careful not to smile. "Of course you are."

Nori's huge baby eyes flashed to him. "Then why can't Allie give me a koala? She promised, and I want it more than anything."

The passion in his son's voice caught Lorne by surprise. "But you have so many toys already."

"I don't have a koala from Australia."

Lorne winced inwardly but kept his face impassive. So that was what this was all about. He dropped an arm around his son's small body and pulled him close, reminding himself that as well as crown prince, Nori was still a baby who missed his mother. "Did talking to Miss Carter remind you of your mama?" he asked carefully.

Nori's full lower lip quivered, and his shoulders trembled under Lorne's hand, but he didn't cry, eliciting a pang of empathy in his father. How many times in his own youth had Lorne fought to contain his emotions because of his position? "It's all right to admit that you miss your mama, you know," he said softly. "You're very brave but when we're alone you can tell me how you really feel."

Nori turned lambent eyes to him. "You won't mind if I cry a bit?"

Lorne shook his head. "Not even if you cry a whole swimming pool."

Nori looked at the vast expanse of water beside them and

gave a shaky laugh. "Nobody could cry that much," he said in the tone of "shows how much you know."

Thinking of his own loneliness that stretched back to well before they lost Chandra, Lorne wasn't so sure. Chandra had never been the companion he had hoped for, but she had been Nori's mother, and the child was entitled to mourn her loss. "How much do you think you might cry then, a bathtub full?"

Solemnly Nori extended his baby hands about shoulder width apart. "Maybe this much."

"That's quite a lot," Lorne agreed. "But it's all right. Cry that much if you want to. And remember, you can always talk to me about mama, or about anything."

"Even about koalas?" Nori said, his eyes brightening with hope.

Lorne restrained a sigh. Had he been as persistent as Nori at the same age? "Yes, even about koalas," he conceded heavily. "While we're on vacation, why don't we visit the zoo and you can see a real koala?"

Nori's eyes shone. "You mean it? Can Allie come, too? She said I should call her Allie and she knows all about koalas."

Wondering at how easily his son had made friends with their guest, Lorne was aware of a feeling very like envy gripping him. He shook his head. "Alison has other things to do besides entertain you on her holiday."

Nori's tiny chin jutted out. "She'll come if I order her to."

Lorne suppressed a smile. "Not if I catch you first." Only the day before, he'd found a soldier marching pointlessly up and down the inner courtyard because Nori had ordered it. Then had followed a serious father-son talk about the responsibilities of being royal. "Didn't I explain to you about giving orders?"

Nori squirmed uncomfortably. "Yes, Daddy. 'S not

much fun being king if you can't make people do what you want."

"That's exactly why Carramer doesn't have a king," Lorne explained. "A long time ago in our history, a king made his people's lives miserable with his orders. When his son became ruler, he promised never to call himself king to remind himself and his heirs not to treat the people as badly as his father had done."

"I won't make anybody miserable," Nori agreed impatiently. He had heard the story before and understood the point his father was making. "I just want Allie to come to the zoo with us. I like her, don't you?"

"I don't know her very well," Lorne evaded.

"If she comes, you could get to know her."

His son would make a good negotiator one day, Lorne thought wryly. "Very well, she can come if you want her to." It would add to the fiction that she had been taken on as a companion to Nori, he told himself, wondering at the way his heartbeat suddenly picked up speed. It had nothing to do with the prospect of spending time in Alison's company, he assured himself. After Chandra, getting involved with any woman, particularly another Australian, was the last thing he needed.

The knowledge didn't stop a flood of raw emotions from surging through him until he gripped the marble coping of the pool, his fingers whitening with the strain. "How about we get on with your swimming lesson now?" he suggested, hoping Nori wouldn't hear the tension in his voice.

His son was too distracted to notice. "After the lesson, can we go to the zoo and see the koalas?"

Lorne shot an involuntary glance at the windows of the Rose Suite overlooking the pool. "Alison isn't well enough to go anywhere today. Perhaps tomorrow if Dr. Pascale says it's okay."

As his son mumbled a reluctant acceptance, Lorne

thought he caught a glimpse of movement at one of the windows and shook himself mentally. Alison Carter was a temporary distraction, nothing more. Taking her with them to the zoo was unavoidable if Lorne was to keep his word to Nori. But if the doctor approved, she would return to her hostel in Allora afterward and that would be that.

Forget about her, Lorne ordered himself and slid into the pool. He felt like a poker being plunged into ice water. Steam practically hissed off him, and he knew the heat of the morning had little to do with it.

Watching Lorne with his son, Allie felt a rush of admiration. He was the ruler of his country, with all the responsibilities that entailed, but he still found time to give his child a swimming lesson.

This afternoon, after sleeping late, eating the light meal that was brought to her room and taking a leisurely bath in the vast bathroom adjoining her bedroom, Allie felt refreshed. She was still tired from her battle with the serpent yesterday but at least her vision was unclouded.

Yesterday she had wondered if she'd exaggerated the impact of the magnificent man who came to her rescue. Today she knew she hadn't. Lorne de Marigny was every bit as prepossessing as she'd first thought. She had reached this conclusion before she knew who he was so his effect on her had nothing to do with his position.

She chewed her lower lip thoughtfully. Why couldn't she have been rescued by an ordinary Carramer man, then she could have enjoyed his company, maybe even a holiday romance? The thought flashed through her mind, startling her with its unexpectedness. There could be no holiday romance with the sovereign ruler of the island kingdom.

She was amazed he had allowed her to stay at the villa, although she recalled it was on doctor's orders. Not that she imagined Lorne de Marigny taking orders from anyone unless they coincided with his own wishes. He was the kind of man who naturally led rather than followed. If he *had* been born a commoner, he would still have been a leader, she sensed. Men like Lorne stood out from the crowd no matter what their station in life.

This perception of him should have been at odds with the gentleness he demonstrated with his son in the pool. The sight reminded her of a lion and its cub. Lorne showed strength when it was warranted and paternal care when it was needed. The fanciful image brought a rueful smile. Lion, indeed! What were lions if not merciless hunters who pulled down living prey on the run?

He had looked at her as if she was potential prey, she recalled with a slight shiver. It wasn't fear, more like—she refused to identify her response as pleasure. He was unlikely to feel any such thing after the way she had interrupted his holiday. The sooner she left the royal villa, the better.

It was hard to make herself believe it. She didn't want to, she acknowledged with a flash of insight. The obvious trappings of royalty didn't attract her as much as the warm family feeling she observed between Lorne and Nori. Toddlers could be a handful at the best of times, but Lorne looked as if he genuinely enjoyed interacting with the child.

When Nori did something amusing, Lorne's laughter reached her as a warm sound that tingled all the way to her toes. She wrapped her slender arms around herself in an instinctively defensive gesture. Toe tingling was all very well if the man was available and interested, but Lorne was neither.

A discreet knock on the outer door of her suite startled her. In response to her soft acknowledgement, a maid entered carrying clothes over one arm. "His Highness saw you at the window and requested that you join him at the pool," the maid relayed. "I was instructed to bring a selection of bathing things for you to choose from."

From the woman's deferential manner, Allie gathered that refusing was not an option. Her bikini wasn't among the choices on offer, she also noticed. Was it too brief for the prince's royal sensibilities, she wondered wryly? The maid hardly seemed like the appropriate person to ask.

"Thank Prince Lorne for me and tell him I'll be down as soon as I've changed," she agreed. After her experience yesterday she had thought she wouldn't want to swim again for a long time, but the weather was too hot and the pool far too tempting. Her eagerness had nothing to do with wanting to be a part of the inviting family scene below her, she told herself.

Lorne was swimming laps by the time she emerged from the villa. She had chosen a one-piece swimsuit that was as modest as her white bikini had been revealing. The high cut of the legs was the only remotely provocative feature. Over the ultramarine-colored suit she had slipped a filmy cover-up in a combination of ultramarine and Moroccan gold swirls. Raffia slip-on scuffs protected her feet from the sun-heated marble tiling around the pool. Finding things to fit her had proved remarkably easy because the maid had brought each garment in several sizes.

Huge seagrass umbrellas provided shade, and she sat down on a lounger under one of them, breathing in the exquisite ginger-scented air. Nori's swimming lesson appeared to be over because there was no sign of the child. Her gaze went almost involuntarily to the figure plowing up and down the length of the pool. The only sound was the beat of Lorne's arms and legs as he sliced through the water.

He was good enough to swim competitively, she thought, riveted by the sight of his smooth progress that left hardly a ripple in his wake. No wonder he was so muscular if he made a habit of exercising so strenuously. Watching the rhythmic kicking of his long legs and the pistonlike arc of his arms made her feel limp.

He made her feel limp for a lot of reasons, she thought, not least being his overwhelming masculinity. A man among men indeed. It would have been easy to fantasize that he had invited her to join him because he found her equally fascinating, but she knew it wasn't the case. Being a good host was probably bred into him from childhood. No matter how reluctant he might be to have her company, he would accept it rather than appear inhospitable.

One thing she had learned in her short stay on Carramer was that hospitality was considered a cardinal virtue. She had already received invitations to share meals with a number of families she had done no more than talk to on the beach, so she supposed the monarch could do no less, regardless of his personal feelings.

Knowing she was here on sufferance did little for her mood, and she was frowning when Lorne emerged from the water. "If you still feel unwell, perhaps you should return to your room and let the doctor take a look at you," he said when he saw her expression.

She started to get to her feet in deference to his position but he waved her back down. "The doctor came to see me half an hour ago," she informed the prince. "He said I'm fine to get up as long as I don't overdo things."

The prince slung a towel around his broad shoulders to catch the moisture beading his honey-toned skin. "Then we must see to it that you don't overtax yourself. The whirlpool tub might be safer for you than a strenuous swim. I was about to head there next myself so you can join me."

The thought of sharing a hot tub with the prince was thoroughly alarming. "I'm fine right here," she said with a furious shake of her head.

He picked up the hesitation in her voice, and his look

challenged her. "Afraid of me, Alison? You weren't yesterday."

"Yesterday I didn't know who you were."

"And now?"

"Now I know you're the boss around here, I don't know how I should behave toward you, Your Highness."

He frowned darkly. "Yesterday you were itching to call me Lorne. Why not start now?"

She was sure her astonishment showed on her face. "How did you know?"

"You forget how well I know the Australian character. You even refer to your prime ministers by their first names. You can't be that much more intimidated by a prince."

Want to bet? she thought furiously. He obviously had no idea of the impact he had made on her long before she knew his title. Insisting on using it would be a dead giveaway so she nodded. "Okay, Lorne it is, as long as it doesn't get me thrown into a dungeon or my head chopped off."

"Such a beautiful head belongs right where it is, on your shoulders," he said without missing a beat. "In any case my palace at our capital, Solano, has no dungeons. For those, you would need to visit my brother, Prince Michel, who governs Isle des Anges. Although it's called Island of the Angels, the island was used to exile criminals centuries ago, and the dungeons remain as historical curiosities. You should see them, as a visitor, of course," he added.

She gave a slight shudder. "No, thank you. I once visited the former convict settlement of Port Arthur in Tasmania and couldn't get out of the cells quickly enough. The walls seemed to be impregnated with the hopelessness of the poor souls who were incarcerated there."

"I think Michel would agree with you. When we were boys, our younger sister, Adrienne, dared us to go into the dungeons, and Michel said much the same thing."

The thought of Lorne having a brother and sister, let alone playing with them as a boy, made him far too human in her estimation. As well, the image of him teaching his little son to swim was still fresh in her mind. "I hope it makes him a benevolent governor," she said quickly.

"Unlike his older brother, you mean?"

Benevolence was not a quality she would readily attribute to Lorne. She bridled, stung that he could read her so well on such short acquaintance. "From what I hear you are a popular monarch."

"But not popular with you," he divined with the same uncanny accuracy.

The feeling was probably mutual, she reminded herself. She was uncomfortably aware that her nationality reminded him of his late wife. But for the doctor's insistence that she rest, she was sure she would be back at the hostel in Allora by now. "I'm well aware that I'm here on sufferance," she said. "You saved my life yesterday, and I'm grateful, but we both know you don't want me to stay any longer than necessary."

"Agreed," he said with a coolness that cut to her core, although it was no more than she had expected him to say. "However, there is a complication."

She regarded him curiously. "Yes?"

"Nori has taken a liking to you, perhaps because you remind him of his mother."

She felt her eyes start to mist and automatically lowered her lashes. "This morning he told me he misses his mother since she died."

"Just over a year ago now," Lorne supplied tautly, his raw tone confirming Allie's suspicion that he didn't want her around because she reminded him of what he had lost. She felt even worse when he added, "Your talk of koalas stirred memories for my son."

She lifted her gaze to him, not caring if he saw the moistness in them. "I assure you it wasn't my intention. He's a delightful little boy. I wouldn't have said anything to hurt him deliberately."

The prince's features hardened perceptibly. "If you had, you would have me to answer to."

She released the breath she had been unaware of holding. "Is there any way I can make it up to him?"

"There's a way," he said shortly. "Nori obviously likes your company. I spend as much time as I can with him but affairs of state are no respecter of vacations. You could agree to become his companion and ensure he enjoys his holiday a lot more."

Indecision gripped her. Lorne was asking her to stay for his son's sake, not for himself, she understood. But what about his disturbing effect on her? From first meeting his impact on her had been considerable. Of course, he would be busy working and she wouldn't have to see much of him, she told herself. The thought should have reassured her, but for some reason it had the opposite effect. "What about his tutors or the nanny someone mentioned, can't they help?" she asked.

The prince gestured dismissively. "They cater for his physical needs, not his emotional ones. You are the first person he has taken to since his mother died. After speaking with you, he finally admitted to me how much he misses her. Previously when I've tried to talk about it with him, he has—what is your expression—clammed up on me."

A frisson of pleasure rippled through Allie at being able to help the little boy, until she reminded herself that she had come to Carramer to enjoy freedom from responsibility, not to take on new ones. "I don't know," she demurred.

His expression turned cold again. "I realize you would prefer to be carefree and unfettered, but is it so much to ask, that you act as a companion to a lonely little boy? So

the doctor can't accuse me of overworking you, I would
allow you a generous amount of free time with no other
duties to burden you, and you would be well paid and ac-
commodated.''

Refusing would be a poor way to repay him for rescuing
her, she thought. It was so unfair. If only the prince knew
how much she had been asked to shoulder in her twenty-
six years, he wouldn't ask her to take on more now. Then
she thought of Nori, so appealing and so lonely despite his
father's devotion and the attention of a small army of staff.
Lorne was right, it wasn't so much to ask under normal
circumstances.

On the other hand, she could resume her vacation as soon
as the prince returned to Solano, she told herself. She was
only delaying her plans, not postponing them indefinitely.
At some level she recognized that it was the same rationale
her mother had used to persuade Allie to go to teachers'
college and help support the family instead of attending art
school, but Allie pushed the thought aside. She was a free
agent now and that included the freedom to take on whatev-
ever commitments she chose.

First she needed to know how long she would be expected to defer her plans. "How long does your vacation
usually last?" she asked.

"A month. We arrived earlier in the week."

Given the sparks flaring between them, and Lorne's obvious dislike of her, a month seemed a dangerously long
time to spend under his roof. On the other hand, how often
did one get an opportunity like this? "Would I be able to
paint in my free time?" she asked warily.

He nodded, thinking that the studio he had created in the
forlorn hope of interesting Chandra in a hobby to keep her
happy would finally be of some use to someone. "I had a
studio set up for my late wife, and you would be welcome
to use it since it remains virtually untouched."

As a shrine to his wife's memory? The thought made Allie uneasy but she pushed it away. Having the use of a well-equipped studio meant she wouldn't need to spend her limited funds on art supplies, and she would be earning a salary so she would be able to extend her stay in Carramer for much longer.

A knot of excitement formed inside her. It had nothing to do with the prospect of working for the most powerful man in the country, she told herself, unsure how honest she was being. She was under no illusion that working for Prince Lorne would be easy but it would not be dull.

"If you think I'm qualified, I'll do it for Nori's sake," she conceded, wondering if she was out of her mind. It came to her that Nori had less to do with her desire to stay than the man in front of her, although he was the last person to want her around for his own sake.

"You have already demonstrated your compassion for my son and that is all I require," he informed her. "My security people will want to check out your background, but you don't strike me as the terrorist type."

"You never know, I could have had a bomb hidden in my bikini yesterday," she said flippantly, using humor as a defense against her confused feelings. She wanted to stay, when it was the last thing she should do, and she was afraid the reason was right in front of her.

"You shouldn't joke about such things," he reproved, bringing her down to earth with a jolt. "These days security must be taken seriously. However discreet the guards, they will have you in sight whenever Nori is with you."

The thought of being under constant surveillance sent a shiver through her. "Is that really necessary?"

"It is for your own safety and that of the crown prince."

Lorne's abrupt tone reminded her that from now on they were on a different footing. "It's going to take some getting used to, Your Highness," she said, deliberately using his title in token of her new status.

His expression softened fractionally. "It can still be Lorne when we are alone." But his next words shattered the momentary sense of rapport. "There is one more condition."

She felt herself tense. "And that is?"

"Inevitably, my son will want you to talk about Australia. You may do so honestly but without embellishment, and you will not encourage the impression that your country is in any way superior to his own. Is that clear?"

What did he think she was? "I'm a qualified teacher. I would never do such a thing," she said in genuine outrage. "If you have doubts, perhaps we'd better rethink the whole idea."

She jumped to her feet, forgetting the loose raffia scuffs that slid from under her on the wet marble coping. Moving as swiftly as a cheetah, Lorne was beside her in seconds, his strength saving her from falling.

As he hauled her away from the water's edge, she was caught against the muscular wall of his chest. His eyes blazed with annoyance, but the heat in them only made him look more attractive. A woman could drown in those obsidian depths, she found herself thinking. A woman could also have her head turned by the strength of the arms encircling her. For a heady moment she relived the fiery brand of his kiss and wondered if he was about to do it again. How would she feel if he did?

But he put her away from him with a firm gesture. "As a teacher you should know better than to make sudden moves on a slick surface."

She should also know better than to let her thoughts run away with her, she chided herself silently. "I'm still a little unsteady on my feet," she said, not wanting him to know that it was caused by his closeness today, rather than the events of the day before.

At once his impatience turned to concern. "I'm not surprised after what you went through. I suggest you return to your room and rest a while longer, while considering my proposal."

The last thing she needed was time to think things over and possibly come to her senses. "I've agreed to stay and I will. I won't even wear my Crocodile Dundee hat around Nori."

The prince fixed her with a regal look of disdain. "In your peculiarly Australian way, I take it you are acceding to my wishes."

She drew a steadying breath. "I believe that's what I said."

"Then welcome to the royal household." He took her hand, his long fingers twining through hers. She felt her gaze narrow and her breathing become shallow, as if the prince had done much more than touch her hand. A warmth spread through her. She was staying for his son's sake, not because he wanted her to, she reminded herself in a bid to quench the internal heat. It worked, and the flames subsided, but she was left with a sense that as long as she was around Lorne de Marigny, they could flare up again at any time.

Chapter Four

Allie found it strange having a public place almost to herself. The zoo director had closed the park to the public for two hours while he conducted Lorne and his party on a private tour. The prince had thanked the man warmly enough, but the slight tightening of his expression told Allie that he would have preferred far less fuss.

Nori had no such reservations. With the boundless energy of a four-year-old he skipped eagerly from one enclosure to the next. Allie loved the way his huge eyes shone with delight as he was shown the animals by the keepers who waited beside each enclosure.

Watching Nori made Allie feel younger and more carefree. "He's having the time of his life," she told Lorne who followed his son at a more restrained pace. "Anyone would think it's the first time he has visited the zoo."

"It is," Lorne surprised her by saying.

She knew her astonishment showed on her face. "But every child needs to go to the zoo. It's a rite of passage." She remembered vividly the excitement of her own first visit to Sydney's Taronga Park Zoo when she was three. The thrill of being allowed to throw a fish to a sea lion at feeding time had remained with her for years. Her spirits lifted automatically at the sights, sounds, even the smells of zoos to this day.

It probably explained why she felt so lighthearted on this occasion, she told herself. She refused to think Prince Lorne could have anything to do with it.

"You are, of course, referring to ordinary children," the prince observed mildly, but she heard the rebuke in his tone.

He had no need to remind her that Nori wasn't ordinary. "He's still a little boy with a child's normal needs and desires," she pointed out, adding on a sudden surge of curiosity, "Didn't you love the zoo when you were his age?"

A fleeting shadow darkened the prince's eyes, then was gone. "I had...other priorities."

Priorities like learning how to run a country instead of running and playing, she thought. Her imagination painted a picture of Lorne at Nori's age, up to his ears in books. She couldn't believe it had been an entirely happy experience. "You must have been positively grim."

Hearing the slight note of reproach in her voice, he frowned. "No doubt I was. Why, every morning the servants would dress me in my miniature ermine-trimmed robes and I would go to the state rooms for my lessons, only coming out to understudy my father at official functions."

"Very funny," she muttered, catching on. "I suppose you slept in your little crown, too."

He shook his head, the challenging light dancing in his dark gaze belying his serious expression. "Sleeping in a crown tends to dent it."

"So what did you do for recreation?" she persisted. She didn't doubt that even as a boy he had been well aware of his duty, but surely there had been room for some fun in his life?

"I had plenty of free time with my brother and sister," he assured her. "Our favorite game was chess."

She almost choked. "Chess? What about ball games or hide-and-seek."

He was teasing her again, and she had fallen for it, she realized belatedly when a faint crinkle around his eyes betrayed him.

"There's no better place for hide-and-seek than a palace with hundreds of rooms," he continued. "One of Adrienne's favorite escapades was riding her bicycle down the Great Hall, much to the annoyance of the housekeeper."

Adrienne was his sister, she recalled. The picture of the three royal children playing together in the palace should have been charming, but it struck her as oppressive for some reason. Then she understood why. Where was the stimulation of playing with other children and having everyday experiences like visits to the zoo? She could see the benefits in Nori's shining eyes and rapt behavior.

Before she could open her mouth to argue, Lorne's look silenced her. "My childhood was what it was. It can't be changed now."

He could change things for Nori, she wanted to say, but his expression told her the discussion was at an end. "Must be nice to be the boss," she muttered under her breath. "You get to win every argument by royal decree."

"Unlikely, now that I have you around to point out the error of my ways," he said, evidently having caught her mutinous aside.

"If you don't want to listen to my ideas, why *do* you want me around?" she couldn't resist asking.

The question had been nagging at her. Since arriving at the summer palace, she'd seen that Lorne spent more time with Nori than many parents who didn't have a country to run. She had also met the capable nanny who saw to the child's personal welfare.

Lorne could hardly want Allie to stay for the sake of her health. The palace doctor had given her the all-clear only that morning, although she hadn't cared for his warning that she was dangerously run-down and should take things slowly. Other than that there were no lasting effects from her near drowning. So why did Lorne want her in his household?

She wanted it, too, she acknowledged to herself with total frankness, but was it because of the little prince or his charismatic father? She had never met anyone remotely like Lorne de Marigny. His power was undoubtedly attractive, and he was also capable of great passion, as she had found out when he'd kissed her during her recovery. Like her childhood memory of the zoo, some experiences were so special that they branded you indelibly. She suspected that Lorne's kiss was one such experience. As if to prove it, her heart pounded wildly just thinking about it.

The kiss had meant little to him, she recognized. He had done it merely to show her who was boss, but the effect on her was much more enduring. Every time they spoke, she was unwillingly reminded of the spine-tingling sensation of his touch and the fiery pressure his mouth had exerted against hers.

The mere thought sent waves of warmth coursing through her. She could blame it on the heat of the day, but on what could she blame the frantic way her nerves leaped every time he came near?

It was unnerving to say the least, especially as it was becoming obvious that his closeness to his son meant their paths were going to cross far more frequently than she had anticipated. So much for thinking she could avoid him.

She wasn't even sure she wanted to.

Alarmed by the trend her thoughts were taking, she pretended rapt interest in a colony of monk seals frolicking in a man-made imitation of their wild habitat. For a moment she felt like the seals, caged and subdued by forces beyond her control. She felt a totally irrational urge to open the gate and free the wild sea creatures, as if by doing so she could free herself.

This wasn't the vacation she had planned when she came to Carramer. After years of taking into account everyone's needs but her own, she had looked forward to pleasing herself, eating and sleeping when she felt like it and painting the hours away.

Now she was about to be bound by a royal routine more demanding than anything her mother or sister had ever imposed upon her. All because she hadn't had enough sense to stay out of dangerous waters.

This was crazy, she told herself. She wasn't Lorne's captive. To escape, all she had to do was resign from his employ. He wouldn't be pleased, but what could he possibly do about it? She wasn't one of his subjects, to be cowed by the majesty of his position.

"Giving in so easily?" he asked so quietly that she wondered if he had managed to read her mind. While she was lost in thought they had moved a little ahead of the others, and his lowered tone ensured he wasn't overheard.

She struggled to remember what they'd been talking about. Lorne must mean her insistence that Nori would benefit from having normal childish experiences. If he had mistaken her silence for capitulation, she had news for him.

She lifted her head. "I can't do much else, can I, *Your Highness.*" Deliberately she gave his title an emphasis that he could read as defiance if he liked. Let him see that but for his position she would gladly argue her point with him—and maybe even win.

His dark gaze allowed no such possibility. "It was Lorne yesterday," he reminded her easily. "And in any case, in deciding what's best for my son I was speaking as a father not a ruler.''

She refused to concede that he was right. The fluttering of a pulse at her throat didn't help. His hands were at his sides, but he might as well have been touching her from the way her skin tingled and her breathing became fast and shallow.

Zoo staff and Lorne's security people paced them at a respectful distance, but for a giddy moment she felt as if she and Lorne were completely alone. "How can you know what's best for him when you admit you didn't have a normal childhood yourself?" she asked, annoyed to hear her voice sounding rusty as if from lack of use.

There was a long pause, filled with the cries of the colorful Carramer parrots squabbling in the leafy canopy over their heads. Finally he said, "Why do you care so much?"

Since waking up in his villa she'd asked herself the same question without much success. "As a teacher, I don't like to see any child unhappy," she said, wondering if he sensed that it was only part of the truth. The other part had more to do with her response to Lorne himself.

His brows flattened and his expression sobered. "You think my son is unhappy?"

You asked for this, she thought, bracing herself. "Not unhappy exactly. He has everything a boy could possibly want and there's no doubt that you love him."

It seemed hardly possible but the prince's steely gaze intensified. "Why do I sense a *but* coming?"

She quailed before his scrutiny but kept her chin up. "Because there is. Nori is four years old. In the last two days, I've watched him have swimming lessons, and I'm sure he has lessons in all the academic subjects, but what he needs are lessons on how to be a carefree little boy. Apart from the moment when he came tearing down the beach looking for you, this is the first time I've seen him act like a normal four-year-old.''

Lorne lifted one finger as if to touch her chin before he let his hand drift back to his side. His gaze went to her mouth, and she felt a tremor grip her. If he had actually tilted her chin up in order to press his lips to her mouth, the effect couldn't have been more electrifying. ''Now you understand why you're here,'' he said in a husky whisper that reminded her of a voice heard in a sexy dream.

How could a man affect her so physically without even touching her? she asked herself in a daze. Even while they were discussing his son, Lorne managed to make her feel as if the discussion was far more intimate. Pity help her if he ever actually did whisper sweet nothings in her ear. From the melting away she felt now, she knew her defenses would be next to nonexistent.

She was the last person he would whisper intimacies to, she reminded herself almost angrily. They *were* discussing his son, and it was only her own febrile imagination that insisted on reading more into his words.

She forced herself to focus on Nori. It was the coward's way out, but she sensed that retaining Lorne's respect depended on her not letting him see how vulnerable she was to his brand of charm. To him she was a means to an end.

''You hired me to play with Nori?'' she asked on a note of frank incredulity.

''To play with him and to care about him. You've just told me that in your professional opinion, it's what he's in danger of missing,'' he reminded her.

''Surely it would be more appropriate to invite playmates to the summer palace,'' she suggested. Acting as a paid companion was one thing, but what Lorne was suggesting sounded alarmingly like a mother substitute.

She would need time to decide how she felt about that. He gave her none. ''The decision is made. Since Dr.

Pascale has cleared you as fit, you will have sole charge of Nori's entertainments. You can start tonight by reading him bedtime stories and playing with him—as you so confidently assert he needs. I will leave the choice of future activities to your professional judgment as long as he derives as much enjoyment as possible from this vacation.''

She felt as if she was in the eye of a hurricane with a storm raging around her on all sides. What on earth had she gotten herself into? She felt annoyed with herself for not insisting on discussing the kind of work Lorne expected his son's companion to do before she accepted the job. She had pictured a kind of teaching role, rather than the close, personal arrangement Lorne was proposing. At the least it meant much closer dealings with him than she had bargained for, and the prospect alarmed her more than a little.

"You don't need a companion for your son. You need a wife," she snapped. As the comment slipped out, she saw his face turn thunderous. She would have given a lot to be able to take it back, but it was too late. What was it about Lorne that provoked her to such rashness?

"I had a wife. I have no need of a replacement," he reminded her coldly.

Because he had loved her so much, Allie assumed. "I'm sorry," she whispered. "I didn't mean—"

"You meant exactly what you said, but you're wrong," he said, cutting across her stammered apology. "There is no longer any room in my life for that kind of relationship."

What kind *is* there room for? The question flashed into her mind, but this time she was able to stop herself from giving it voice. Saying any such thing would suggest an interest in him that was way too intimate. Already the kind of commitment he wanted from her was too personal for her peace of mind.

It wasn't that she didn't find little Nori delightful. He

was an enchanting child, and a job that largely entailed playing with him hardly amounted to work at all. But given Lorne's electric effect on her, being around him in anything but a strictly professional capacity seemed like playing with fire.

Then she stiffened her spine. She was not going to renege on their agreement just because of some attraction she had probably conjured up out of her imagination. The doctor had said she was tired and run-down so it wasn't surprising if she was inclined to be more fanciful than usual.

She had tutored children who were every bit as needy in their way as the crown prince was without getting in over her head emotionally. She could do it again with Nori.

But what about his father? a small inner voice insisted.

Her voice betrayed her tension as she said, "In that case, I'd better catch him up and apply myself to my duties, hadn't I, Your Highness?"

He caught her arm, spinning her slightly off balance. "There's no need to pretend a subservience you obviously don't feel. I think I prefer you with fire in your eyes and a touch of acid on your tongue."

She couldn't help herself. "Fire and acid can be destructive if not handled carefully."

The prince locked eyes with her. "Then I shall have to make sure I handle you carefully, won't I?"

Against her will she was shaken by the promise redolent in his words. It reminded her yet again that as well as a monarch he was very much a man. Her defenses rose automatically. "You've just finished warning me that there's no room in your life for that kind of involvement."

His mobile mouth remained sternly set, but his eyes flashed a challenge. "I said I wasn't in need of a wife. I didn't say there's no room in my life for other kinds of what you coyly describe as involvement. Unlike English, the Carramer language has eleven different nouns for your one word, each one describing a specific kind of relationship."

She couldn't resist asking, "How many kinds of relationships can there possibly be between two people?"

The expression in his eyes confirmed the audacity of the question. "In my language they range from *amere,* the most casual association, what you would probably call a brother-sister relationship, all the way to *amouvere* and that, I assure you, is definitely not appropriate between brother and sister."

Her throat felt tight but she refused to swallow and let him see the effect his words had on her. The singular kind of resonance she shared with Lorne made her wonder if they had already moved beyond *amere,* perhaps from the first moment when he lifted her into his arms on his private beach.

He hadn't elaborated on exactly how two people became *amouvere,* and she swiftly rejected the images her mind insisted on supplying. They all revolved around herself and Lorne, and that was impossible.

Before she could gather her wits and respond, he had moved ahead of her and was devoting his attention to his son. She told herself he had taught her the words purely as theory, not because there was any chance of her experiencing the relationships they described. It didn't stop her internal temperature from soaring as she imagined the possibilities.

She clenched her teeth and reined in her imagination with an effort. Lorne had an uncanny way of making her thoughts go off on these kinds of tangents. Was it a royal speciality, or the province of all alpha males? Either way she found it unnerving.

She quickened her steps, disliking intensely the way he had managed to leave her several paces behind him and Nori. Although she had asked for it with her attitude, she didn't care for the lonely way it made her feel. It also reminded her uncomfortably of all the times she had been required to put others' needs before her own.

Ahead of her, Lorne and Nori approached a tall timber enclosure bearing the outline of a familiar animal on a plaque at the entrance. Her breathing quickened involuntarily as she watched Lorne duck beneath the low-beamed entrance. Lord, he was big.

With the little boy holding tightly to his hand Lorne also looked heartstoppingly tender. She found him attractive, Allie had to admit. Very attractive. For a brief moment she wondered what it would be like to hold his hand and be his—what was the word he had used?—his *amouvere*.

Of course she wasn't going to be in Carramer long enough to reach that stage with him. Or any of the other ten stages leading up to it, she promised herself. For the first time in her life she was accountable to no one and she was determined to keep it that way. Helping Lorne with Nori was a side trip on her life's highway, nothing more. All she had to do was remember it.

Telling herself it was because she wanted to see Nori's face when he finally encountered a koala, she hurried after Lorne.

She caught up with them walking up a timber ramp that spiraled around a grove of Australian eucalyptus trees, ending level with the treetops. The distinctive scent of eucalyptus oil reminded Allie so much of home that a pang gripped her. She was glad when Nori distracted her by excitedly pointing out a family of koalas, some chewing contentedly on shoots of gum leaves and others rolled into sleepy balls of fur in the forks.

The little boy could hardly contain himself as he raised limpid eyes to his father. "Can I take one home?"

Over the child's head, Lorne's expressive gaze locked with Allie's and she sensed his regret at having to refuse the heartfelt request. "We have no gum trees for them to feed on."

"We could grow some," Nori persisted.

A smile tugged at the corners of Lorne's mouth, contagious in its warmth. She found herself smiling back reluctantly, caught up in the moment as if she belonged here. She shook off the feeling. "Koalas only eat the leaves from one special kind of gum tree," she told Nori. "It would take years to grow enough trees for them to live on. You wouldn't want them to be hungry, would you?"

Nori chewed his lip, torn between his desire to have a koala of his own and his obvious wish not to hurt them. "I suppose not."

Allie ruffled the child's dark hair. "As we came in, I noticed a poster about the zoo having a sponsorship program. Maybe your father could arrange for you to sponsor the koala enclosure."

Nori looked dubious. "What does sponsor mean?"

"It means we help the zoo by sending them money to take care of their koalas, so in a way it's like having some of your own," Lorne supplied. "Would you like us to do that?"

"Really?"

Lorne exchanged looks with Allie over Nori's head. "I'll have my aide set the wheels in motion as soon as we return to the summer palace."

Nori leaned as far over the railing as he could. "Don't worry, Mr. Koala, I'm going to help take care of you so you'll always have enough gum leaves to eat."

Allie was still smiling an hour later as they were being whisked back to the summer palace in the prince's limousine. Exhausted by all the excitement, Nori had fallen asleep with his head resting against her and her arm encircling him.

She was slightly sunburned, and her legs tingled from the walking they'd done and the effort to keep up with the prince's long strides. Seated opposite her, he was talking softly on the car phone. It sounded like official business, and he didn't notice when she sneaked a glance at him, surprised at the tug she felt around the region of her heart.

She made herself look away to her young charge. It wouldn't do to let herself get too beguiled by Lorne's attractiveness. She needed to remember that there was only one man in this family in whom she could afford to be interested, and it wasn't Lorne. She had already seen how heavily his duties weighed upon him, even while he was on vacation. Any woman who shared his life would have to be there for him while shouldering her own burdens, and Allie had had quite enough of responsibility for a while.

When the limousine turned into the gates of the villa, she glanced again at Lorne. He had finished his call and was watching her. "It never lets up for you, does it?" she asked him.

His wide shoulders lifted expressively. "One is never really off duty, if that's what you mean. It doesn't bother me."

But it would bother someone who hadn't grown up in the royal family, she was willing to bet. Allie found herself wondering how his Australian wife had coped but choked off the thought. It was really none of her business. "I hope you didn't mind me making the suggestion about sponsoring the koalas," she ventured.

He shook his head. "It was a good idea, although in future it may be wise to discuss such notions with me before voicing them to Nori."

The rebuke was mild enough but it rankled for some reason, although she accepted that he was justified. As a teacher she knew enough to clear her ideas with her pupils' parents first. "I'll keep it in mind," she said tautly.

He leaned slightly forward, the move bringing him alarmingly close to her in the confines of the vehicle. "Sulking, Alison? It doesn't become you."

"I'm not sulking," she denied hotly, feeling her face begin to heat. "But I thought with the wealth you're reputed to possess, sponsoring a koala enclosure wouldn't cause you any difficulties."

He gave a deep sigh. "It isn't a question of money but of priorities. The royal family could easily be criticized for putting animal welfare before, say, a new preschool or medical facility."

"I didn't think in those terms," she conceded. "But you're right. Luckily I won't be here long enough to cause you too many problems."

"You've already caused me more problems than one woman has any right to do," he said, surprising her.

"Because of the way I blundered into your life?"

He nodded. "Partly. But mainly because of the gossip your presence at the villa has evidently triggered. I was just talking to a member of my government, and he informs me that there is already considerable speculation about your role in my life."

Warmth spiraled through her, making her want to uncurl like a cat, but that would bring her into contact with the prince's long limbs so she kept her legs still. "I could end the gossip by leaving the villa and going on with my holiday," she offered, refusing to consider how hard it would be to do.

She was almost relieved when Lorne's silence rejected her offer.

Chapter Five

Where was it written that a head of state also had to be an accountant, Lorne asked himself irritably. Why didn't he simply rubber-stamp these wretched documents instead of forcing himself to sift through the dense language of the ledger keepers? The answer was simple. He didn't believe in walking away from his responsibilities, however onerous they might be.

He chuckled, imagining his father's tut-tut of disapproval at Lorne's mutinous thoughts. Of course, his father hadn't had to contend with the increasingly complex global world of today. During his father's reign the most difficult problem had been convincing his people to welcome the tourists who wanted to come in ever-increasing numbers to Carramer's once isolated shores.

That one tourist in particular might be preying on Lorne's mind, he hated to think, but he couldn't seem to prevent his thoughts from wandering to Alison Carter. She had lived at the summer palace for a week now, and it seemed that the difficulty of keeping his mind on affairs of state had existed for precisely a week.

It wasn't only because she was beautiful. Feature by feature, he knew many women who were more conventionally beautiful than his son's new companion. For a start, compared with the sleek dark hair common to women of Carramer, Alison's tawny mane curled much too extravagantly around her shoulders, giving her a wild, untamed look.

Then there was the way she moved with the unconscious grace of a dancer. Unaware that the prince was within earshot, the gardener had wolf-whistled at her, Lorne recalled wryly, remembering the rueful way Alison had smiled back at him, while Lorne would ensure steps were taken to prevent the gardener repeating his discourtesy. For a fleeting moment Lorne had wished himself in the gardener's shoes, able to indulge his feelings for once without thinking of his position.

What was it about her that turned his thoughts in such reckless directions? Apprehension swirled through him until he willed it away. He wasn't the gardener, nor some callow island youth to have his head turned by a pixie of a woman just because she possessed eyes the color of the sea in storm.

They were stormy enough when they turned on him, he couldn't help recalling. She seemed to delight in rebelling against his authority at every opportunity, but contrarily he found their verbal sparring oddly stimulating. She acknowledged no man as her master, making him sorely tempted to prove himself the exception.

Was it the lure of forbidden fruit? he asked himself. As the ruler of Carramer, few things were forbidden to him, it was true. Perhaps he should allow himself more time in her company until he found the flaws she must possess. Then perhaps he could shake off the restlessness that plagued him whenever he thought of her.

He could also be playing with fire. On closer acquaintance, she might prove even more intriguing. In frustration he slammed his flattened palm down on the desktop, wincing as pain jarred all the way to his shoulder. He had kissed the woman. How much closer did he want to get?

Dangerous train of thought, he told himself as heat immediately flooded through him. His mind insisted on picturing Alison in a skimpy white nightdress, standing tremulously beside the bed in the Rose Suite, her long, slender legs on the point of buckling. Yet she had continued to defy him until he gathered her into his arms and claimed her mouth with his own.

He had meant to prove that he outmatched her on every level, but something had gone wrong. Instead of bending her stiff neck, she had responded with a bone-deep passion that he could swear surprised even her. It had certainly surprised him almost as much as his own response.

The moment he took her in his arms his need for mastery had fled, replaced by a much more urgent and old-fashioned biological need. If he was honest with himself, he had wanted to make love to her more than he had wanted anything in a long time. It had taken every ounce of restraint he possessed to put her to bed by herself and walk out of the room.

This was getting him nowhere. Feeling as restless as a hunting tiger, Lorne stood up and stretched. His office overlooked the pool and gardens, and he paced to the window and looked out. At this time of day Allie was usually to be seen playing with Nori in the gardens below. Concern stabbed through him as he surveyed the deserted expanse of lawn.

Telling himself it was no more than normal concern for his son's well-being, he picked up a house telephone. Surely Alison had not kept Nori inside on such a glorious afternoon? "Where is Miss Carter and my son?" he asked an aide.

The answer was not the one he expected to hear, and he

had to resist the urge to slam the receiver down. He glanced briefly at the figures cluttering the computer screen but knew he was far too angry to concentrate anymore today. He paused only long enough to shut down the program before setting off to find Allie and demand an explanation.

Why wasn't the painting working the way it had in her mind's eye? Furiously Allie scrubbed at the canvas with an oily rag until she had obliterated most of her afternoon's work.

"Lorne de Marigny, you are the most elusive man I have ever tried to paint," she muttered at the muddy remains. The canvas represented the latest of several disastrous attempts to paint the prince as she saw him in her mind, the embodiment of the Man of Sparta and Athens archetype, who was said to be able to combine both artist and warrior with equal ease.

Before erasing the portrait she had managed to capture the outward magnificence of the man, but his inner qualities eluded her, along with his easy masculinity. Why it should matter so much to her to get it right she wasn't sure, she only knew that it did.

She stared at the canvas. Even with the details obliterated the remaining outline suggested a man to be reckoned with. She touched a paint-stained finger to where the face had been, idly tracing what had been Lorne's features and were now only a ghostly vestige. Sighing, she picked up her brush.

It was hard not to work on his mouth without recalling the feel of it covering her own. She set her teeth and tried to approach her task objectively, suspecting she failed miserably. How did artists ever manage to paint their lovers? she asked herself. Something of what they shared had to come through in the painting, and if what they shared was as stormy as her interactions with Lorne up to now, no wonder she was blocked.

He wasn't her lover, she reminded herself furiously. He was the absolute monarch of his country, and she was his employee. Maybe he kissed all his new employees and she was reading far too much into a brief contact that he had already forgotten ever happened. If she had any sense she would try to do the same.

It didn't help, and after a few more attempts she set the brush aside. "Girl, I think you've finally met your match."

"I couldn't have put it better myself."

Shocked, she whirled around to find Lorne himself angled across the studio entrance. His wide shoulders all but filled the doorway, her artist's eye noted almost automatically. The studio was spacious enough, but she had moved the easel closer to the door to make the most of the natural light, and it brought her so close to Lorne that awareness of him sent little shocks pulsing through her.

She wanted to move away, put some much-needed space between them. When he was this close, she had trouble ordering her breathing and her thoughts. She wasn't sure whether it was because she didn't like having him this close or because she liked it too much. Either way his proximity disturbed her more than she cared to admit.

He looked, she couldn't help thinking, exactly the way she wanted him to look in her portrait, except for the fury she was startled to see in his eyes. "Is something wrong?" she asked in sudden alarm. "Is Nori all right?"

"He's with his tutor, as you well know," Lorne ground out.

His anger caught her off guard. "I know. I arranged it myself."

His dark brows came together ominously. "So you could dabble in your painting without having him under your feet?"

Getting angry wasn't the exclusive province of royalty, she discovered as she felt her hackles rise. "In the first place Nori is never under my feet. I love the time I spend with him," she said hotly. "I would never shunt a child in my care on to someone else to get him out of my way. And in the second place, I don't *dabble*."

Lorne stalked into the studio and turned a critical eye on the smeared canvas. "What do you call this? Some kind of modern art?"

Resisting the urge to shrink back behind the sheltering confines of the easel, she stood her ground. "I call it a failure," she snapped back. "But it doesn't mean I'm one, at least not yet. I'll keep trying until this portrait comes out the way I want it to."

Lorne's obsidian eyes glowed. "And if it doesn't?"

"Then I may be forced to accept my limitations. But I assure you there are a lot of attempts to be made before I reach that stage."

Thank goodness she had erased the portrait's more recognizable features before Lorne walked in, she thought when he gave a grudging nod of agreement. Was she imagining it or did his gaze hold a faint glimmer of admiration? If there was, it vanished abruptly when he said, "According to his timetable, you are supposed to be with my son, not locked away in a studio letting Nori's tutor assume your responsibilities."

Shock gripped her, rendering her momentarily speechless. Neglecting Nori in order to indulge herself was totally out of character. If she hadn't allowed her family to run her ragged, always putting their needs before her own, she wouldn't have needed the palace doctor's warning that she was endangering her health. Relying on the doctor's confidence, she had explained everything to him, finding him sympathetic and comforting. But for some reason she didn't feel ready to share the details with Lorne.

As a result the prince didn't have any idea of what her life had been like before she came to Carramer. If he had, he would have known that putting herself first was so foreign to her that she recoiled physically from the prince's accusations.

He put his own interpretation on her silence. "If you have nothing to say in your own defense, I must assume I have drawn the correct conclusion," Lorne went on, sounding more disappointed than angry now.

He had taken a step closer, and his breath teased her cheek. She couldn't believe how much it hurt to have him sound so upset with her, especially knowing it was totally unjustified. She also had trouble dealing with his nearness, she realized as her heart began to hammer a response.

She summoned her voice with an effort but still found herself avoiding his gaze. She looked instead at the tanned column of his throat. "I shouldn't have to defend myself," she said huskily. "In my country we believe people are innocent until proven guilty."

"Then you claim to be innocent?"

One strong finger crooked under her chin, and she lifted her head. "Not according to you, Your Highness. Apparently I handed Nori over to his tutor and happily took the afternoon off to please myself. It evidently hasn't occurred to you that there might be another explanation altogether."

At the hurt vibrating in her tone, his harsh expression softened a little. "I would be delighted to hear your version."

His choice of words made her bridle. "I don't have a version. What I have is the truth. Nori's tutor has a sick mother and he needs some time off to take her to the hospital tomorrow morning. Rather than have Nori miss any lessons, he asked if he could tutor your son this afternoon and let Nori and me have our time together tomorrow instead."

It was obvious that such a simple explanation hadn't occurred to Lorne, she saw as his expression underwent a rapid change. His obsidian eyes gleamed and his brows lowered as he digested the new information. "So you decided to use the unexpected free time to paint," he concluded.

"Give the man a cigar," she muttered, so hurt that she forgot momentarily exactly who she was talking to. "How could you think for one minute that I'd put my own interests ahead of Nori's?"

"His mother invariably did."

The admission took some of the wind out of her sails. She had assumed that the prince and his wife had been totally happy together. Another servant had told Allie that the studio had remained untouched since Chandra's death, leading Allie to conclude that Lorne had kept it intact as some sort of shrine to his wife's memory. The thought had been unexpectedly painful. She had only managed to quell her discomfort by taking some deep breaths and rearranging things until she felt more at home.

It had never occurred to her that Lorne's wife might have been a less-than-perfect mother to Nori. Or perhaps Lorne himself had resented the child taking his wife's attention away from himself. No, Allie denied the thought almost as soon as it arose. The prince's devotion to his son argued against any such pettiness. But it did make Allie wonder what else she might have been wrong about.

"I'm sure she had good reason," Allie found herself saying, unsure of what else to say.

"Women invariably have good reasons for their more extreme behavior, at least according to themselves," the prince murmured.

Allie wiped her paint-stained hands on a rag, wondering if his wife had done something to lead him to such a cynical conclusion, or if he was simply biased toward women in general. Perhaps it had something to do with his royal upbringing making him less tolerant of ordinary mortals. "We're not all alike," she said, feeling the need to defend her gender for some reason.

One dark eyebrow lifted in blatant disbelief. "No?"

She gave a sigh of frustration. "Some of us actually have an overdeveloped sense of responsibility."

"You speak for yourself, I assume?"

This was something she wasn't yet ready to admit to him, even if he would believe her. "I'm speaking for many of the women I know," she insisted. "What about all the wives and mothers who sacrifice their own dreams and ambitions in order to take care of their families?"

"If it's what they want to do, it can hardly be called a sacrifice," he insisted.

Lorne might be lord of all he surveyed, she thought, but at that moment she would have loved to hit him with something hard and heavy. Her hand actually lifted from her side until she forced it down again. One did not go around slapping the face of the country's monarch, no matter how much he was asking for it, she reminded herself.

She settled for attacking him with words. "It's easy for you to say from your privileged position."

His eyes flashed a challenge. "It has not stopped you from speaking your mind so far. You may continue."

She tossed her head. "I may, may I? By royal decree, I'm permitted to have my own opinion."

She had made him angry, she saw as a muscle started to work in his jaw. But he kept his gaze level. "Are you deliberately trying to provoke me, Alison? Very well, I admit I was wrong about your motives this afternoon and I apologize. But I strongly suggest you don't try my patience too far."

If he had stopped at the well-deserved apology, she might have kept her fool mouth shut, but the added warning made her see red. "It's generous of you to admit you're wrong about me, Your Highness."

"I didn't say I was wrong about you, only about your behavior this afternoon. Everything you've said so far confirms my original conclusion that you are typical of your gender—hotheaded, totally lacking in respect and quite irresponsible. Unfortunately, my son likes you, so there's not much to be done about it."

She wasn't sure whether to be grateful that Nori appreciated her so much or sorry that the child's enthusiasm had gotten her into this situation. At the same time she felt irrationally annoyed at the reminder that Lorne was only keeping her around to please his son, not because he valued her presence for its own sake.

Resentment, however illogical, flashed through her at the thought. "While we're cataloging my flaws I'm surprised you didn't add that I'm an amoral temptress, as well." As soon as the words were out, her breath escaped in a rush of horror aimed at herself. Something about the man provoked her almost beyond endurance, but why on earth did she have to plant such an outrageous idea in his mind.

His brows drew together ominously. "Since I've already misjudged you once today, I don't want to risk making another judgment without sufficient evidence."

The cynical, slightly brooding way he spoke should have warned her, but she was already so disturbed by Lorne's nearness that it seemed impossible for her to feel any more mercurial. Shows how wrong a woman can be, she told herself later.

It wasn't until his hand came up and rested lightly on the back of her neck that she had any idea what kind of "evidence" he meant to collect. Heat surged through her as his touch sent tingles of sensation down the length of her spine. She didn't want him to touch her, and yet the sensation so weakened her defenses that the denial she should have thrown at him stuck in her throat. "What are you doing?" she managed to whisper.

"Gathering evidence," he confirmed in such a seductively low voice that her remaining defenses threatened to crumble altogether. When he bent his head and his mouth claimed hers, her knees felt like buckling, and it was just as well that his arms were around her, supporting her.

Telling herself it was only for a moment, she let herself savor the taste of his lips on hers while awareness of him throbbed through her like the bass notes of a compelling piece of music. When he lightly caressed her neck and shoulders, a tingling sensation spiraled all the way to her fingers and toes.

As his mouth shaped hers to his needs, her lips opened in automatic response, and the pounding of his fast-beating heart resonated through her body. She had heard of two hearts beating as one, but had thought it a physical impossibility until now. It was extraordinary to discover that she wasn't the only one so strongly affected.

The moment stretched into two then three, then she lost all track of time as the kiss went on and on, drowning her in sensations she could barely assimilate. No one had ever kissed her so compellingly, as if she was the only woman in the world.

He was testing her, she reminded herself with what remained of her reason. Like her family and everyone else in her life, he would use her—whether for Nori or for himself—then let her go when he no longer needed her. She was a fool to let him affect her so strongly.

He sensed the tension radiating through her and lifted his head. "Alison?"

"I don't want this," she managed to say, although everything in her screamed a denial. She did want it, and more if she was honest with herself. But there was no way she dared let him know it.

"I could give you an argument on that," he said, hearing her unspoken truth, anyway. "But I have never yet had to force myself on a woman. I don't intend to start with you."

He let his hands drop, and she stepped back, hoping he wouldn't see how shaken she felt. It would have been the easiest thing in the world to move back into the circle of his arms and let him go on plundering her mouth with seductive ease. To let him slide her cotton shift off her shoulders, the better to caress the lightly tanned skin underneath. It was too hot to wear a bra, so there would be nothing to stop him drinking his fill of her heated flesh.

"No," she denied aloud, feeling her face flame. What was it about Lorne that put such notions into her mind? She had never considered herself a sensual person, preferring to express her deepest feelings through her paintings. But around him, paint seemed a drear, lifeless medium compared to the touch of skin on skin and mouth on mouth.

She hated to think it was why she was having so much trouble bringing his portrait to life, but was afraid it was true. How could a mere canvas convey the power and passion her eyes, heart and mind recognized in Lorne, however unwillingly? She took refuge in evasion. "I...I should go and find Nori. His lesson should be over by now."

His wasn't the only lesson that was over, she recognized, judging by the assessing way Lorne regarded her. "Before you run away, don't you want to know my verdict?" he asked in a voice so low it sent shivers down her spine.

She drew herself up, refusing to let him see how badly his kiss had affected her. Whatever his verdict might be, it couldn't be allowed to matter to her. "I'm hardly running away. As Your Highness has reminded me, I have duties elsewhere."

He gestured dismissively. "They will keep for another few minutes. There's the matter of my verdict to be settled first."

She pretended ignorance. "By now I've forgotten your question."

He gave a laugh that held little humor. "I doubt it, but it's possible, given what I felt from you when I kissed you. But that is in itself an answer, since the question is whether or not you are an amoral temptress."

She hated herself for asking but couldn't resist, as he knew she would, she realized when she saw the amusement dancing in his gaze. Damn him, he had a knack of knowing exactly what was going on inside her. It made her feel transparent in a way that she found distinctly unsettling. "And am I?"

He took his time about answering. "Are you a temptress? Oh, yes, without doubt." He lifted her right hand and lightly grazed her knuckles with his mouth. She felt her throat muscles lock. "As for amoral, I shall reserve judgment until I have more…evidence."

The slight hesitation wasn't lost on her. Retrieving her hand, she faced him, feeling her eyes blaze with the force of her annoyance. "Since giving you that evidence would actually prove the point, I'll have to make sure it doesn't happen, won't I, Your Highness?"

His heavy-lidded gaze settled on her. "Are you sure it's within your control, Alison? Twice now I've kissed you, and twice you could have resisted, but you didn't."

She tossed her head, her chestnut hair streaming around her shoulders. "You're the prince. I can hardly tell you to get lost, can I?"

"Then pretend for a moment that I'm not the prince. I'm Lorne de Marigny, commoner, and I've just kissed you. How do you respond?"

Part of her knew exactly how she would respond, and it didn't bear thinking about. Then there was the part hurt beyond endurance at the way he insisted on misjudging her. It had tempted her before to lash out at him. This time she couldn't stop herself. Before she had the thought fully hatched, she drew back her hand and aimed it at his cheek, putting all her distress and confusion into the blow.

As she pulled her hand away he stopped it in midair, holding her in a grip of iron. She had the feeling that had he exerted slightly more pressure, he could have broken her wrist. He knew exactly how much force to apply to immobilize her without doing any real damage, except to her pride. "I suppose I asked for that," he said mildly.

"You did," she muttered through gritted teeth. In truth she was shocked by how much he had managed to provoke her. She had never slapped a man in her life, regardless of the circumstances. To think she had actually lost control so badly as to strike Lorne proved that he affected her more than any man had ever done. "I'm sorry," she whispered, not sure whether she was apologizing for her anger, or regretting that it was all they could ever share.

He steered her arm down to her chest, trapping it against the hard wall of his body. He was so close that the intake of his breath sounded loud to her ears, and she wondered if its unevenness meant that he was more moved by the exchange than he was letting on.

He looked down at her, so close that she was unable to avoid meeting his eyes. They held anger at what she had dared to do, but also something very like respect. No, she must be imagining that part. But the anger was dauntingly real. "Do you know what the penalty is in Carramer for striking the monarch?" he asked quietly.

A shudder took her, but not at any imagined penalty. He had invited her to treat him as she would any man who had taken liberties with her, so he had asked for what he got. Her reaction had far more to do with his closeness and the hardness in his gaze. All she could manage was a nervous shake of her head.

"You become bonded to the royal household for as long as the ruler pleases," he informed her.

No hint of a smile suggested he was joking, and her stomach muscles clenched in automatic rejection of such a prospect. "You can't be serious," she denied. "You can hardly penalize me for complying with your own instruction."

He nodded as if considering this. "I invited you to speak your mind, but I didn't anticipate such a physical reaction."

Neither had she, if truth be told. She was still shocked by what she had done. The marks of her fingers on his cheek were damning proof of her recklessness. "What are you going to do?"

"I sentence you to two months under personal bond to me. It should be time enough for you to repent your rashness."

Her mouth dropped open. "Two months? I only agreed to work for you for one month."

"That was when you were working for me of your own volition," he snapped out.

She stared at him. "You're serious about this bonding business, aren't you?"

"Try to leave the country and you'll find out how serious," he agreed.

"You mean I'm now a prisoner here?"

"Not a prisoner as you understand it. In our society a person under bond can continue their normal life, but any kind of social activity or travel, even local expeditions, require the bond master's consent."

This was some kind of crazy dream, she told herself, feeling dizzy. "I'm a free woman and this is a new millennium. I refuse to submit to such medieval nonsense."

"There is an alternative," he suggested.

Why was she sure she wouldn't like it? "Which is?"

"You can leave the country, but you will not be allowed to return."

It was the obvious solution, and she should jump at the chance to escape from his archaic notion of justice. All the same, the thought of never being able to come back—of never seeing him again, came the traitorous thought—filled her with dismay.

He still had hold of her hands, and her heart began to beat almost unbearably fast. Two months was not much more than she had already agreed to work for him. It would mean using up almost all the remaining leave time she had budgeted for, and the need to find a new job when she returned home would be even more pressing, but she couldn't bring herself to go. What possible difference could the terms make? "I'll stay, damn you," she said indistinctly.

His look would have melted ice. "Somehow I thought you would."

Chapter Six

"It's great to have someone of my own age living in the royal household," Laura Myss, Nori's nanny, confessed as she poured tea for them both. Laura was a pretty woman of French and Carramer extraction, and Allie liked her enormously. They had developed the habit of enjoying lemon balm tea together each afternoon while their young charge napped.

During these sessions Allie had gradually discovered how much she and Laura had in common, including their love of children. Laura also came from an artistic family and painted watercolors in her spare time, exhibiting them at a gallery in the capital. She had promised Allie an introduction to the owner.

"I'm glad to have you for a friend, too," Allie agreed. "Without you to explain Carramer customs to me I'd be lost."

Laura regarded her thoughtfully. "Customs like the personal bond?"

Allie almost choked on the fragrant tea as she saw from

Laura's expression that it wasn't an idle question. "Why do you ask?"

Laura looked concerned. "In the palace, gossip travels faster than a brushfire. Then it's true that the prince has bonded you to him?"

Allie nodded. "I'm afraid so. I made the terrible mistake of slapping his face and..." She couldn't go on.

Laura blanched, obviously finding it hard to believe that anyone would do such a thing. "What on earth made you slap Prince Lorne?"

"Haven't you ever been so angry at a man that you lashed out at him without thinking?" When Laura looked nonplussed, Allie added, "No, I suppose you haven't. I hadn't, either, until I met the prince."

"And as punishment for slapping him, he placed you under personal bond." Laura frowned. "Such an action is almost unheard of these days, except occasionally between two people who want to show how close they are, then it's known as—"

"*Amouvere,*" Allie put in, her breath escaping in a rush.

Laura reacted in surprise. "You know this word?"

Allie could imagine what Laura would think if she knew that Lorne himself had taught her the uniquely Carramer expression. The more she learned about its meaning, the more sure she was that Lorne hadn't meant it to refer to them in any sense.

The certainty didn't stop heat from flaring deep inside her and traveling along her limbs. She told herself there must be another Carramer word for what she felt every time Lorne intruded on her thoughts, something that meant pure sexual attraction. She felt it every time Lorne was near her. Just thinking about it was enough to set her pulses racing, but she told herself it was a purely physical response. It had nothing to do with the deeper sense referred to locally as *amouvere.*

"I heard the word somewhere," she said, trying to sound unconcerned. "I'm sure it has nothing to do with the prince's plans for me."

Over the rim of her Limoges teacup, Laura nodded. "From what I have read, a bond can take several different forms, ranging from an archaic form of indenture for a certain period, to a form of engagement."

Alarm pulsed through Allie. "You mean engagement as in marriage?"

Laura smiled. "Isn't marriage the ultimate bond?"

"No doubt, but it's hardly likely to be what Prince Lorne has in mind on this occasion."

"All the same, the personal bond is seldom imposed anymore, other than between lovers," Laura said, her expressive fingers fluttering in the air.

Allie remembered Lorne's seriousness when he pronounced her sentence. "Old-fashioned or not, the prince has imposed it now. It means I can't leave his employ for two months."

Laura looked dismayed. "Is it such a terrible prospect? I thought you were enjoying your stay with us."

Allie hated to hurt the other woman's feelings when she was being so supportive. "I am, although I preferred having a choice whether I stayed or not. It's hardly how I planned my visit to Carramer." The discordant feeling of being drawn to the prince against her better judgment was definitely not what she planned, but she kept that part to herself.

"Is the painting not going well?"

Honesty was no problem there. "You know it is. I've never been so productive in my life." The studio the prince had allowed her to use was wonderfully well equipped, once she had rid herself of the sense of intruding on his past. In her free time she had completed some studies of little Nori that satisfied even her own demanding scrutiny. Only the portrait of Lorne himself continued to elude her.

Laura picked up her teacup, a smile hovering on her delicate mouth. "Then perhaps you should look on the two-month bond as a gift from the prince rather than a penance."

Allie sighed, envying Laura's rare ability to look on the bright side of things. Of course she was safely married to her childhood sweetheart. She didn't have to deal with an attraction so powerful that it was almost frightening. Nor with the realization that nothing lasting could possibly come of it. Where Lorne was concerned there was simply no chance of a "happy ever after."

"I'll try," she conceded, seeing from the nanny's relieved expression that the concession pleased her. "What else can I do, now Prince Lorne has dug up your old law to make sure I can't leave until he permits it?" Try as she might to ignore it, the very thought made her throat tighten.

Laura gestured delicately with her teacup. "Are you sure His Royal Highness isn't attracted to you, Allie? Perhaps imposing the bond is the only way he can persuade you to stay until you come to feel the same way."

Hearing the possibility put into words stunned Allie into silence for a moment while she digested it. She couldn't deny how strongly the prince attracted her. When they were in the same room, her senses felt ragged with the strain of *not* imagining him as a lover. Picturing him in her bed was all too easy and far too seductive. She was sure he would make love as potently as he did everything else.

It was the everything else that was the problem. He was a dedicated monarch, beloved by his people and adored by his son. But there was only so much of him to go around. Being good together in bed could hardly make up for having to share him with a whole country.

Annoyed with herself for reacting so strongly to Laura's

suggestion, Allie shook her head. "Even if you're right, and I'm not sure you are, it would never work even if he bonded me to him for life."

Disturbed by the vivid images Laura's idea had conjured up, Allie got to her feet and walked to the carved parapet separating the terraced area from the rainforest garden beyond. Steaming in the afternoon heat, the rainforest looked as tangled as her thoughts.

She turned back to Laura. "He can't be attracted to me. He dislikes everything about me. Sometimes I think he dislikes women in general, probably because he loved his wife so much that he can't bear to think of loving anyone else now she's gone."

Laura gave her a puzzled look. "Where did you get that idea?"

"It's true, isn't it? Why else would the prince keep her studio exactly as it was, except as a memorial to her?"

Laura shook her head. "Sadly, you are wrong. The studio remains as it was because it reminded him of what should have been, so he ordered it locked and abandoned. I worked for them both for a time, and what I glimpsed between them was not love, at least not on the princess's part. She was from your country, and palace gossip said she adored the idea of being a princess but not of performing her expected duties. She was—what do you call it?— a playgirl."

"There's no real female equivalent of a playboy in the English language, but I get the picture," Allie explained, masking her inner turmoil. She had never imagined that Lorne and his wife had been unhappy; the opposite, in fact.

Then she recalled his expression when he let slip that Chandra had not been a good mother. According to Laura, she hadn't been a good wife, either. Was that why Lorne resented Allie so fiercely? Not so much because she came from the same country, but because she seemed to be as irresponsible as his late wife.

She had given him no reason to think differently, she accepted uneasily. She had kept from him the details of her struggle to hold her family together after her father left. He couldn't know that when she should have been thinking about boys, dating and what to wear to dances, she had been worried about her mother's health, her sister's education and how to pay the bills coming in steadily.

If she had been more forthcoming with him, would he have treated her differently? she wondered. No, she didn't want him to treat her differently, she thought on a sudden rush of alarm. For his sake and little Nori's she was sorry if his marriage had been unhappy, but it had nothing to do with her. All she wanted from him was her freedom, and he had managed to deny her that for at least two months.

"You didn't really slap the prince, did you?" Laura asked. The awe in the nanny's voice told Allie she found the idea almost inconceivable.

Still wrestling with her confusion, Allie returned to her seat and poured herself a fresh cup of tea. "Yes, I did, but he deserved it."

"How can you say such a thing? He is the ruler of our country. Whatever he does is the right thing, by custom if not by law."

"Then it's time you updated your laws and customs," Allie grumbled. "He can't go around kissing the hired help just because he feels like it."

She hadn't meant to admit this part to Laura, and it was a measure of how much she had come to like and trust the other woman when it slipped out so easily. Instead of looking shocked as Allie thought she might, the nanny rested a hand on her friend's arm. "Allie, he doesn't make a habit of kissing the hired help, as you call it. To my knowledge he has not looked at another woman since his wife died. If he kissed you, it suggests you are the first woman to re-awaken his male passions."

Allie felt more than a few qualms at this. Surely she didn't want Lorne to see her in a romantic light? The demands made on Lorne, even on vacation, convinced her she wanted no part of royal life herself. If his late wife had felt the same, discovering it only after they were married, it would explain a great deal.

"I'm sure you're wrong," she told Laura, recognizing wishful thinking when she heard it. "He has bonded me to him so I can't leave, but only as—what did you call it?—an archaic form of indenture. No doubt I'm too outspoken and independent for his liking, and this is his way of bringing me to heel."

Laura looked unconvinced. "The prince doesn't generally object to outspokenness. He encourages his staff to speak their minds to help him keep in touch with popular thinking."

Seizing on the change of subject, Allie leaned forward. "Then why don't you tell him that Nori needs playmates his own age? You know it's true." The two of them had discussed the subject before, but Laura had been unable to explain why the prince preferred not to invite other children to the summer palace.

Laura shifted uncomfortably. "It's the one subject the prince resists discussing. I'm not sure why. He will do anything he thinks will make Nori happy."

"Except the one thing we agree the child needs," Allie contributed. "Maybe he doesn't want other children visiting the palace at Solano. But what about while we're at the villa? Things are more relaxed here."

"I haven't brought it up since we got here," Laura admitted unhappily.

Allie immediately regretted pressing her friend. "I know this is difficult for you. He is your prince, after all. What if I raise the question with him? He can't do much more to me than he's already done.''

He could extend her bond by another few months or forever, she thought nervously, but if Laura was right, he wouldn't punish her for offering an opinion... As long as she kept her hands at her sides, she reminded herself with a rueful smile.

Laura seemed to read her thoughts. ''You mustn't try to slap him again, Allie.''

Allie made herself look solemn. ''I'll try not to, but I can't promise anything. He seems to have a knack for getting my back up.''

For once she didn't have to explain the colloquialism to Laura, who smiled. ''In my experience, the only people who can get our backs up, as you put it, are the ones who touch our emotions most deeply.''

Allie sighed. They were back to the prince's effect on her again. ''Laura, he doesn't touch my emotions and I definitely don't touch his,'' she said with exaggerated patience. What he did touch, she wasn't prepared to confess to anyone.

Laura looked unconvinced. ''I believe there is another expression from your literature that fits this situation, something about protesting too much.''

Allie laughed. ''You're impossible.'' Inwardly she wondered whether she *was* protesting too much. Lorne was on her mind a lot for someone she didn't give two hoots about. Sexual attraction only went part of the way toward explaining the emotional hunger he aroused in her. It was so new to her experience that she shied away from it instinctively, but she couldn't pretend it didn't exist.

Another thought gave her pause. If her state of mind was so transparent to Laura, was she an open book to Lorne, as well? She hated to think he knew what effect he had on her, choosing the bonding as a way to keep her close until she admitted it. What would happen if she did? He would be a formidable lover, she had already concluded, the thought provoking unwelcome quivers of sensation deep inside her. She had no doubt he would ensure she gained as much as he did from the experience. But what then?

Despite the temptation, she didn't want a brief encounter even with a man of Lorne de Marigny's caliber, she told herself emphatically. She might be old-fashioned, but she dreamed of a relationship with all the frills, mental as well as physical. She wanted the bond the Carramer people called *amouvere,* she realized uneasily. They didn't think it was wishing for the moon. Why should she?

She pushed the thought away. She could worry about her own emotional state later. For now Nori's welfare was her main concern.

A knock heralded the entrance of a maid, who presented Allie with an envelope bearing the royal crest and Allie's name on the correspondence. Watched by Laura, Allie opened it and read the note curiously. "The prince wants me to join him at a cocktail party he's giving tonight," she said, feeling an unwanted surge of excitement that she quelled hastily. "It will give me the perfect opportunity to talk to him about letting Nori have some playmates to visit."

Laura looked troubled. "It may not be the best time."

"In my experience no time is the right time to disagree with His Royal Highness," Allie said, setting her jaw. "But for Nori's sake, I'm willing to take the risk."

Lorne looked with distaste at the clothes his valet had laid out for him. The crisply pressed charcoal linen pants, starched white shirt and monogrammed cravat were informal enough in keeping with the nature of this evening's gathering, but they were still too formal for his mood.

A man on vacation shouldn't have to dress up unless he

wanted to, he told himself. He had felt much happier getting ready for the evening meals he'd begun sharing with Alison lately, he realized.

He smiled, recalling her reaction when he'd first invited her to dine with him, to hear her report on her day with Nori, he had explained, not sure whether either of them fully believed it.

When she joined him for dinner, tension had radiated out of her as if she expected him to bite. He admired the way she had refused to yield to it, or to him, standing up to him as few people in the kingdom had the courage to do.

Lorne had arrived for dinner wearing a jacket and tie to find Alison in a bright floral dress whose only concession to formality was its ankle length. Noting the frown of disapproval he'd been unable to suppress, she had offered to change, but instead he had removed the jacket and loosened his tie.

Instead of being appreciative, she had laughed lightly, the sound reminding him of silver wind chimes. "That's better. A man on holiday should be able to dress as he pleases," she had said. Only now he connected his own thoughts with her reasoning and his brow furrowed. When had she begun to influence his thinking so strongly?

About to remind her that he wasn't a man on holiday but a prince with duties and obligations, he had checked himself. He knew what she would say and she'd be right. If a prince couldn't do as he pleased, who could? It wasn't as if the country would be any less well-governed because Lorne allowed himself to relax occasionally.

Dr. Pascale had been telling him so without success for years, Lorne reminded himself. Alain would laugh if he knew that it had taken a slip of an Australian woman only a couple of weeks to convince him.

What would Allie wear tonight? Not that he cared on his own account, he told himself. Mindful of her limited selection of clothing and meager budget, he had offered to have some suitable gowns brought to the palace for her to choose from, but she had said stiffly that she wouldn't let him down, if that was what concerned him. He couldn't refute it because he *did* want her to make a good impression, but for her sake, not his. While at the summer residence, he customarily gave several parties to satisfy his social obligations, and he knew far better than Allie how competitive such occasions could become. He didn't want Allie to feel out of place.

For her it would be a novel experience, not the chore Lorne anticipated. For a moment he envied her the ability to see things through fresh eyes, until he drove the thought from his mind. She was in his thoughts far too much lately. Even inviting her to the party was out of character. Only the fact that some of the other guests were Alison's countrymen provided any sort of justification for inviting a member of his staff to a social occasion.

Strange, he pondered. He hadn't given much thought to her nationality lately. She managed to seem so much at home in Carramer. Playing outdoors with Nori so frequently had kissed her skin with gold and added becoming highlights to her chestnut hair. She could have passed for someone from Isle des Anges, where the women were generally fairer skinned and lighter of hair.

The fantasy vanished as soon as Alison opened her mouth, he thought, feeling a frisson of annoyance ripple through him. Why did she have to be so infernally contrary and outspoken, as if she positively enjoyed crossing swords with him?

She was as bad as his late wife, he told himself as he knotted the cravat at his throat with a savage gesture, having dismissed his valet so he could be alone with his thoughts. Neither woman knew the meaning of the word *respect*.

Not quite true, he added mentally. When they'd argued during dinner, and Lorne's reasoning outweighed Alison's, she had gracefully conceded the point to him. He couldn't imagine his late wife doing so.

Of course Alison had struck him, and his anger stirred again as he recalled the fury sparking in her gaze before she lashed out at him. He was slightly chagrined at having put her under personal bond before he'd had time to think it over, but it would set a poor example if he withdrew the sentence now.

Dr. Pascale would call it stubborn pride and would no doubt urge him to release her. Lorne knew it was probably wise, but something held him back. She needed to learn that one couldn't slap the country's ruler and get away with it. Keeping her nearby for a few weeks longer had nothing to do with his decision.

Chapter Seven

The maid who had introduced herself as Myrna finished dressing Allie's hair and stepped back to admire her handiwork. "You look beautiful, Miss Carter, just like a princess."

Allie felt her jaw drop open as she stared at her reflection in the mirror. Myrna had pulled her hair back from her face, catching it in a cascade of curls at her nape and securing it with a heart-shaped tortoiseshell clasp. A few strands had been left loose to curl around her face. The effect was indeed regal but also incredibly feminine. "I never knew I could look like that," Allie whispered in awe.

Myrna frowned reprovingly. "Like so many beautiful women, you underestimate yourself, miss."

"Call me Allie, please," she told the maid yet again. "How can you say I'm beautiful when you've worked for a woman like Princess Chandra?"

Myrna made a face. "I should not speak ill of her now she's gone, but I can tell you she had no inner beauty." She fussed with Allie's curls. "You have both loveliness on the outside and a generous heart within, the true test of beauty."

"Stop, you'll give me a big head," Allie protested.

The maid frowned. "Your head will grow?"

"Not literally. It's an expression for becoming conceited," Allie explained hastily, anxious for a change of subject. "We'd better hurry. I don't want to keep the prince waiting."

Myrna's smile became secretive. "He will not mind if the wait is worth it." Before Allie could object she insisted, "Have you not noticed? When he looks at you, his eyes hold the glow of a man who finds a woman attractive."

Confusion coiled through Allie. She had seen the prince look at her with annoyance and frustration when she didn't do things his way. By no stretch of the imagination could she interpret it as attraction, and she said so.

Myrna shook her head. "Perhaps he is not ready to let you see what is in his heart."

And perhaps the maid was letting her fantasies run away with her. Allie was certain the prince didn't feel in the least romantic toward her. It was true he had kissed her, but in the heat of battle, not tenderly as between lovers. How would she feel if he ever did? The way her breath caught and her pulse picked up speed was an answer in itself.

She lifted her chin and straightened her back. It wasn't going to happen. She was as bad as the maid, letting herself get caught up in fantasy. "You'd better finish my makeup so I can get dressed," she said in a voice barely above a whisper.

Myrna insisted on making up her eyes, something Allie seldom did for herself. The final effect was extraordinary. The maid had smudged her eyelids with sea-green powder and rimmed her eyes with kohl so they looked larger and more luminous somehow. Her skin already glowed from her hours in the sun, needing no further cosmetic help. As a finishing touch, Myrna colored Allie's lips with a carmine pencil.

"Moisten them for me," the maid requested, standing back to admire her handiwork.

Allie ran her tongue across her lips and was startled at how full and sexy they looked. Like an invitation, she couldn't help thinking. She hoped Lorne wouldn't read it and think it was meant for him. She debated whether to ask Myrna to try a less enticing lipstick then brought her head up in defiance. For possibly the first time in her life she felt truly beautiful. If Lorne couldn't cope, that was his problem.

"You've done a wonderful job," she told the maid. "You must give me a few tips sometime."

Myrna smiled. "I'll be glad to, but my simple skills can only enhance beauty, not create it. The other staff say you are a painter of considerable skill. Do you take credit for the appearance of your subject, or for bringing their special qualities out on canvas?"

Allie lifted her hands in mock surrender. "You're right, I give in."

Myrna lifted a small, framed photograph off the dresser and studied it. "Is this your family?"

Allie nodded. "That's my mother on her wedding day a couple of months ago. The man is my new stepfather."

"And the bridesmaid must be your sister. There is a resemblance, but she looks younger."

"Nicole is five years younger than me," Allie explained. "I practically brought her up after our father left us."

Myrna nodded and returned the photo to the dresser. "You see? I was right, you do have a generous heart. Have you heard from your family since you came to Carramer?"

"We exchange letters." Allie didn't tell the maid that her sister's letters were litanies of complaint about the difficulty of studying while holding down a part-time job, as

Here's a **HOT** offer for you!

Get set for a sizzling summer read...

with **2 FREE ROMANCE BOOKS**
and a **FREE MYSTERY GIFT!**
NO CATCH! NO OBLIGATION TO BUY!

Simply complete and return this card and you'll get **2 FREE BOOKS** and **A FREE GIFT** – yours to keep!

Visit us online at
www.eHarlequin.com

- The first shipment is yours to keep, **absolutely free!**

- Enjoy the convenience of Silhouette Romance® books delivered right to your door, before they're available in stores!

- Take advantage of special low pricing for **Reader Service Members only!**

- After receiving your free books we hope you'll want to remain a subscriber. But the choice is always yours—to continue or cancel, any time at all! So why not take us up on this fabulous invitation, with no risk of any kind. You'll be glad you did!

315 SDL C4FD

215 SDL C4FC
(S-R-OS-07/00)

Name:	
(Please Print)	
Address:	Apt.#:
City:	
State/Prov.:	Zip/Postal Code:

◄ DETACH HERE AND MAIL CARD TODAY! ▼

The Silhouette Reader Service™ —Here's how it works:

Accepting your 2 free books and gift places you under no obligation to buy anything. You may keep the books and gift and return the shipping statement marked "cancel." If you do not cancel, about a month later we'll send you 6 additional novels and bill you just $2.90 each in the U.S., or $3.25 each in Canada, plus 25¢ delivery per book and applicable taxes if any.* That's the complete price and — compared to cover prices of $3.50 each in the U.S. and $3.99 each in Canada — it's quite a bargain! You may cancel at any time, but if you choose to continue, every month we'll send you 6 more books, which you may either purchase at the discount price or return to us and cancel your subscription.

*Terms and prices subject to change without notice. Sales tax applicable in N.Y. Canadian residents will be charged applicable provincial taxes and GST.

if Allie didn't know from her own experience. Her mother's letters were more cheering. She and Greg were happy. He refused to pander to her when she was ill, but was utterly devoted to her when she was well, her mother wrote. The idea made Allie thoughtful. Perhaps she should have adopted the same approach with her mother, rewarding wellness rather than illness. Of course she had been a child herself when her father left, so such an approach was beyond her experience.

She blinked at her reflection in surprise. Why had such a simple idea never occurred to her before? Given her age and limited experience, Allie had done the best she could for her mother and sister when they needed her. Now the rest was up to them.

She felt lighthearted suddenly and smiled at Myrna as the maid held out the dress Allie was to wear to the cocktail party. Lorne had offered to send up some clothes for her to choose from, but she had refused. It was bad enough knowing she was bonded to him for the time being. Having him provide an expensive gown for her, as well, struck her as way too intimate for comfort.

Myrna shook out the dress. "Wearing this, you will look a vision for His Royal Highness."

"I'm not dressing to please the prince, or any other man," Allie denied heatedly, not sure why she was protesting so strongly. "Where I come from, women dress to please themselves."

Myrna smiled knowingly. "Perhaps that is what you tell yourselves but surely all women dress to please a man?"

Allie felt momentarily stunned. Was she being less than honest with herself? At home in Australia she rarely used makeup, and the last time she had put her hair up was for a high school formal. Could she honestly say that none of this was to please Lorne? It was hard enough facing the truth herself. She wasn't about to admit as much to the maid. "He is the prince," she said grudgingly. "I had better stay in his good books, hadn't I?"

Myrna smiled. "Looking as you do tonight will certainly put you in what you call his good books. I hope so. Since his wife was killed there has been no woman in his life."

"Maybe so, but I have no intention of applying for the position," Allie insisted, again hearing in her head the line about protesting too much. This conversation had gone far enough for her peace of mind. She held out her arms for the dress. "Let's get this over with."

Since she had anticipated spending most of this holiday painting, Allie had packed only one good dress, a simple black crepe sheath a colleague at school had copied for her from an Aloys Gada original Allie had admired in a fashion magazine.

As Myrna helped her into it, Allie couldn't help noticing how the cutaway design of the shoulders showed off her light tan. A keyhole opening in the front exposed rather too much décolletage for comfort, but it was well within the bounds of decency. It was probably her recent discussion with Myrna that left Allie feeling so exposed.

The dress fell in a flattering A-line to midcalf. Keeping up with Nori's boundless energy, Allie had lost a little weight, she noticed, as the maid settled the dress over her hips. As a result the reflection greeting her in the antique cheval mirror looked positively fragile.

It was probably for the best. Lorne had told her that the other guests at tonight's affair all belonged to the local nobility, so there were bound to be masses of designer clothes draped over figures honed in expensive private spas.

Allie couldn't help smiling, picturing being asked for her beauty secret and confessing that it was playing with an active four-year-old on a daily basis. Naturally she couldn't help thinking of Nori without an image of his formidable father popping into her head. It wasn't true that she had dressed to please him tonight, but she couldn't suppress a feeling of anticipation.

So far he had seen her mostly in casual clothes, without much makeup, usually romping with his little son. He had asked that she join him for dinner each night so she could report on Nori's day, but as they were all on holiday, she drew the line at dressing up. She wasn't conceited enough to take credit for the change, but Lorne had become more relaxed about his appearance in the short time she'd known him. How would he react to seeing her dressed like a princess?

It was the maid's fault for putting the idea into her head, she told herself heatedly. She didn't care how he reacted. No matter what the maid imagined Lorne would see when he looked at Allie, he was her employer, nothing more.

All the same her smile lingered as she left the Rose Suite.

"What do you find so amusing?"

She jumped, startled to find the prince practically outside her door where she almost cannoned into him. He put out a hand to steady her, and fire raced through her veins, ignited at the points where his fingers rested on her bare skin. She shook herself mentally. She would have to stop reacting so strongly to his slightest touch.

He must have been making sure she was ready. Or had he planned to escort her to the party himself? She pushed the notion away as unlikely and slightly disturbing, although she wasn't quite sure why. "I was lost in thought," she dissembled.

His gaze lingered on her newly enhanced eyes and ruby lips with every sign of approval. "You looked like a woman who was thinking about a man," he suggested in a caressing baritone that made the fine hairs on the back of her neck lift slightly.

It was so close to the truth that she felt her eyes widen. She couldn't possibly tell him the whole truth so she settled for part of it. "I was thinking of a man, but he happens to be four years old."

He inclined his head. "How conscientious of you to be concerned about Nori during your free time. I am pleased."

He didn't sound pleased. He sounded disappointed, she thought. Had he expected to be the male occupying her thoughts? He was, but she refused to give him the satisfaction of admitting it. His ego was large enough already.

"You leave me no choice," she said without missing a beat. "I asked Laura Myss about the meaning of a personal bond, and she kindly explained your customs to me. Since you and I hardly share the sort of bond that precedes marriage, I gather I'm indentured to you for the next two months. I may not have a choice about it, but I don't have to like it."

His eyebrows canted upward as he digested this. Goodness, he looked amazing, she thought as her breathing quickened involuntarily. He wore a dinner suit of midnight-blue, and the satin lapels gleamed in the light from the antique sconces lining the hallway. An impossibly white shirt almost made her eyes hurt. Or was it thinking of the hard-muscled body it concealed that forced her to look away?

"You seem certain that servitude is the only kind of bond I have in mind for you."

Her head jerked back and her gaze collided with his. Big mistake. His look was so—*predatory* was the only possible word—that she had to stop herself from licking her lips in response. No sense giving him ideas. Her appearance had obviously given him enough of those already. She never should have let Myrna make her up so provocatively when she was already skating on thin ice with him.

She clenched her hands together tightly, wishing for a purse or some other object she could cling to for support. Not Lorne, never Lorne.

He had no right to steal her hard-won peace of mind, she told herself fiercely, and she wasn't going to let him get away with it. She had earned a respite from responsibility. Royal or not, he wasn't going to take it away from her. "What other kind of bond can there be between us?" she asked as haughtily as she dared.

Slowly he lowered his magnificent, leonine head, bringing his mouth closer to her ear. "I'll let you know as soon as I make up my mind."

Her blood boiled. This had gone far enough. She never should have slapped him, and she wished with all her heart that she had shown more restraint even though he provoked her more than any man she had ever known. But he'd taken his revenge by bonding her to him. It didn't mean he was entitled to treat her as some sort of chattel.

In this century even a bonded person must have some legal rights in Carramer. Whatever the local customs were, she wasn't one of his subjects, to be disposed of at his whim. Being forced to stay in his employ for longer than she'd anticipated was bad enough. What would she do if he expected more from her? No. She refused to consider it. "When you've made up your mind? Now wait a minute—"

"No, you wait a minute." His words silenced her with the force of a whip crack. "Your impulsiveness got you into this situation. Would you care to try for a longer sentence?"

Mutinously she glared at him. "Surely your laws don't let you pass sentence on someone merely because they annoy you? Don't you have courts of justice in this country?"

"The highest court in the land is the crown," he told her implacably. "Still thinking of appealing your sentence?"

"There wouldn't be much point, since the court could hardly be impartial in my case," she snapped.

He crooked a finger under her chin and tilted her head

back. "You tempt me to demonstrate how partial I could be where you are concerned."

She wrenched her head to one side, concealing from him how much such a demonstration appealed to her. She strongly suspected how he would go about it, and the mere thought of being in his arms again sent eddies of sensation whirling through her.

He didn't have to kiss her to have an effect on her, she realized. He had a way of arousing her with no more than a look or a touch, something she had never experienced before. She didn't want it now, but he was so close that she felt overpowered by the sheer physicality of his presence.

This couldn't go on. She took refuge in anger and tossed her head back. "Go ahead, then. You're the prince, the absolute master of everything. You may be able to subdue me with legal chicanery and the force of your position, but you'll never subdue me in any other way."

He gave a deep sigh that might or might not signify regret. "Again and again you tempt me to prove you wrong, Alison. When I touched you a moment ago, your reaction was all the proof either of us need that it could go much, much further. You might offer a token resistance, but that's all it would be, because even now your body craves what your words deny."

Odd that he should use a word like *crave*, summing up her feelings so exactly. She did crave his touch, when all common sense argued against it. Lorne wore a look of knowing what she was thinking, and her anger returned. She drew herself up, wishing for the extra few inches that would make them eye to eye.

Perhaps not.

Settling her gaze on the firm line of his jaw, she swallowed with difficulty. "Is that the sentence you have in mind for me, Your Highness? To be a love slave, without the right to refuse you?'' In spite of herself, her heart lurched in her chest. She told herself the response was caused by aversion, but suspected it wasn't the whole story.

Her fixed gaze noted the slight softening around his mouth. "In spite of what you evidently believe, I am not so starved for female company that I have to compel a woman to share my bed. No, I placed you under personal bond to teach you respect for the crown, if not for the man wearing it. It looks like I have a lot of work to do yet."

"None of this was in the job description when I agreed to act as your son's companion," she reminded him huskily.

His midnight look raked over her. "Neither was slapping the ruler of Carramer."

She pulled in a deep breath, unwilling to let him see how close she felt to doing it again. Heaven knew what the sentence for that would be. "You provoked me by asking me to treat you as an ordinary man. Then when I did, you pulled rank on me. You can't have it both ways," she said as calmly as she could.

A frown carved a furrow into his forehead. "Do you usually slap the men in your life?"

It was out before she could stop herself. "Only the ones who get to me."

As soon as she said it, she felt consternation sweep over her. Had she really made such a revealing admission? "I mean the ones who annoy me beyond endurance." She tried to salvage the situation. "It was the first time I've ever done such a thing."

It was too late, she saw by the devilish gleam in his eyes. "So you admit I'm the first man to 'get to you' strongly enough to provoke such an extreme reaction?"

She set her jaw. "I admit nothing, except that I can't compete with your power and position, Your Highness."

She invoked his title in a desperate attempt to put some

emotional distance between them, but his expression told her immediately that her strategy was wasted on him.

So she was surprised when he nodded agreement. "Very well, for tonight only I decree what you Australians call a level playing field. You will be treated neither as employee nor bonded woman, but as the equal of any guest at the party. We shall see what difference it makes."

Stunned into silence she could only incline her head, her thoughts in turmoil. His decree made her shockingly aware that she had been using her lowly status as a shield against the powerful attraction he exerted for her. Why on earth had she goaded him into changing the rules even for one night? Where it might lead hardly bore thinking about.

There was no time to argue now. The hubbub coming from the rooms below them told her that most of the party guests had arrived. Earlier Laura Myss had informed her that protocol required Lorne to enter only when all the guests were assembled. It wouldn't do to keep the monarch waiting.

Allie had little option but to accept the arm Lorne offered and let him lead her into the lion's den. It was difficult not to think about how solid his arm felt under her hand. The outline of muscle and sinew was strong even through the exquisite fabric of his suit. Pampered monarch he might be, but he kept himself in amazing shape.

She distracted herself with the thought that being permitted to regard herself as his equal for the night might make it easier to raise the subject of playmates for Nori. The prince could hardly pull rank on her in defiance of his own decree.

The touch of Lorne's hand might have activated a whole battalion of butterflies inside her, but she willed them to behave and kept her expression outwardly serene. Since she couldn't change the situation, she might as well enjoy it, she decided as they made a slow descent of the sweeping staircase.

Tomorrow would be soon enough to deal with reality. Tonight she was Cinderella being escorted to the ball by an honest-to-goodness prince. So what if the fantasy had to come crashing to a halt at midnight? In her case the prince would have no need to search for her if he wanted her. He would know exactly where to find her, no glass slipper required.

No starry-eyed romance, either, she reminded herself. She should remember that the Cinderella fantasy was just that, a fantasy, with no prospect of a happy ever after. Lorne's previous marriage had seen to it.

Well, it was fine with her, too. After supporting her family for the past few years, she didn't need the crushing responsibilities that came with a royal marriage. A glittering evening with Lorne at her side was more than enough, or so she tried to assure herself.

They paused outside the ballroom while the orchestra struck up the first few bars of the Carramer national anthem, and Allie wondered yet again how honest she was being with herself. Tonight she was likely to find out.

She felt Lorne's eyes on her and managed a shaky smile. "Ready?" he mouthed. Thankful for his steadying arm, she nodded. Making an entrance was not something she'd had much practise at.

He made it easy for her by letting her know by subtle touches when the anthem was drawing to a close and when to wait while he acknowledged the applause that greeted their arrival.

She was aware of the buzz of speculative talk directed her way and was suddenly glad that Myrna had taken such pains with her appearance. Most of the other women looked as if they could give the modeling profession serious competition. The glitter of costly jewels was dazzling, the gowns only a fraction less so. Allie drew a deep breath. If this was an informal occasion, a formal one must be a doozy.

"I thought you said this was a casual affair," she murmured for his ears alone.

"Relax, you are the envy of every woman here," he assured her sotto voce.

Only because she was on his arm, she was willing to bet. She suspected that her dress had been assessed by label and approximate price the moment she walked into the room. Just as well this was only for one night. She could carry off the fish-out-of-water routine for one night, but a longer commitment was another matter.

The thought helped her to relax as Lorne led her to a group she was pleased to see included the palace doctor. "Good evening, Alain," she greeted him enthusiastically.

The doctor smiled back. "I'm delighted to see you looking so well, my dear."

"Better than well—stunning," Lorne corrected his friend.

She felt the warmth surge up her cheeks. If Lorne wasn't careful, he would start rumors he would find difficult to allay. She debated whether to point this out, then decided it wasn't her problem. He was the one who had to remain in Carramer long after she was safely back in Australia.

The thought brought an unexpected pang, startling in its intensity. It wasn't as if she wanted to remain in Lorne's kingdom, was it? Her experience so far was a long way from the carefree painting holiday she had anticipated. By all rights she should be eager to leave the place and all its problems behind.

She glanced at Lorne, wishing there was a way to free her hand gracefully from where he still had it tucked under his arm. Short of starting an unseemly tug-of-war, there wasn't much else to be done. She fixed her attention on Dr.

Pascale who had an arm around an attractive gray-haired woman.

The doctor performed the introductions and Allie was delighted to learn that the woman was Helen Pascale, the doctor's Australian wife.

"How lovely to hear a familiar accent," Allie said.

"I lost most of it a long time ago, dear," Helen told Allie, her kindly eyes twinkling. She shifted her gaze to Allie's hand, tucked cozily in Lorne's. "Perhaps I won't be the only expatriate in royal circles for much longer."

"I shan't be staying. I'm only visiting for—" Confused by the warmth she could feel emanating from Lorne, Allie went blank on exactly how long she was bonded to the prince.

"Two months," he supplied smoothly. Was he reading her thoughts now? "But you only came for a vacation, Helen, so anything is possible."

The older woman laughed. "This is the Rainbow Kingdom, after all. Miracles have been known to happen, so I wouldn't book your return ticket just yet." She leaned closer. "Carramer has a way of casting a spell that makes people want to stay on and on."

She was committed to staying, but not for the reason Helen imagined. For one giddy moment Allie considered slipping away from the party and flying out of Carramer while her deal with Lorne still held. He had suspended the bond for tonight, so in theory she was free to do as she wished.

Except that she was afraid she was already doing it.

Chapter Eight

Allie had seen enough of the royal residence to know that the rambling granite villa could easily provide the set for a movie based on a Jane Austen novel. But this was the first function she had attended here, and the grandeur of the Painted Salon was breathtaking.

The vast room took its name from a magnificent mural by a famous French artist that dominated the longest wall. The painting echoed the splendid ocean view the villa enjoyed from two sides. It was so realistic that Allie was tempted to try stepping through it to the seascape beyond, anything to escape the curious eyes of the sixty or so other guests.

She couldn't speak more than a few words of the Carramer language, but she knew enough to recognize the word for Australian, and her own name, hovering on dozens of lips. Most of the glances directed at her were openly friendly and curious, but a handful were downright hostile, notably from a couple of older women chaperoning younger clones of themselves.

Mothers hoping Lorne would look favorably on their daughters? Their furious looks almost made Allie laugh aloud. Not only was she no threat to their ambitions, she didn't even want to be. If they only knew, Lorne had probably elected her as his escort because she was the only single woman in the room with no designs on him.

Her restless gaze took in the chandeliers, fine antiques, Aubusson rugs and a fireplace as large as a room in many normal households. It was all very grand and beautiful, but it wasn't the home Allie imagined for herself.

She could hardly fault the ambience. By day the long French windows provided a view of a manmade lake brimming with water lilies and surrounded by century-old Tallow wood trees, their branches echoing with birdsong.

On this fine, tropical night, the doors stood open, and the sumptuous drapes were drawn back. Flaming torches invited guests to step out onto the marble-paved terrace beyond. She looked at it longingly.

If Lorne had been her escort for real, they could have wandered outside and savored the beauty and sensuality of the fragrant night air. He might have pulled her into the circle of his arm, letting her rest her head against his shoulder while he murmured sweet nothings into her ear.

For a moment she could practically feel his firm, warm arm, and her heartbeat began a wild tattoo, until Helen Pascale's soft voice shattered the vision. "The nights here are so beautiful. They're one of the reasons I decided to stay."

Allie made an effort to gather her wits. Letting herself fantasize about Lorne was not only foolish but dangerous. When her two months' bond was up, she would be more than ready to return to Australia and let someone else take her place as Nori's companion. Even if a romance with Lorne was advisable, the reality would never fit Allie's vision. She had only to look around her to see what royal life was really like.

For a moment she envied Helen the love of a man she didn't have to share with a kingdom. "I don't suppose the doctor had anything to do with your decision to stay?" she said wistfully.

Helen colored prettily, an unexpectedly girlish gesture for a woman Allie guessed must be over sixty. "He may have had something to do with it. We met when I was a nurse working at the hospital in Solano as part of an exchange program. Alain was on the staff. At first I dismissed it as a holiday romance, but as soon as I got back to Australia I knew it was the real thing. He helped me to obtain a full-time position at the hospital, and I never thought of leaving Carramer again."

"Don't you miss your home and family?"

Helen gave a decidedly Gallic shrug. "I visit my relatives or they come to see me, but my home is wherever Alain happens to be." Her keen gaze sharpened. "I suspect I'm not telling you anything you don't already know, Alison."

"Call me Allie, please. I'm not sure I know what you mean."

"Just now, when you were lost in thought, your expression looked familiar, although I couldn't work out why at first. When I first met Alain, I saw the same expression on my own face when I looked in a mirror. It's the look of a woman who's so busy falling in love that she doesn't realize it's happening until it's too late."

A white-gloved waiter offered them canapés on a silver salver, saving Allie the need to answer right away. Both women chose minute portions of bread topped with perfectly formed roses of smoked salmon. As if sensing Allie's discomfort, Helen said, "One good thing about having royal connections, the catering is fabulous."

Allie nodded, welcoming the diversion. "When I came

to Carramer, I never imagined myself working for a prince and living in a palace.''

"This is only the summer residence. Wait until you see the real palace at Solano," Helen enthused. "And don't tell me you aren't staying long enough. If I know Lorne, he won't let you escape as easily as you think. When he walked in with you, he also wore a look I recognized. I remember seeing the same look on Alain's face soon after we met. Sort of ambushed, but happy about it.''

Allie almost choked on the salmon. Much more of this and she would start believing that Lorne could really care for her. It wasn't true, and even if it was, Allie didn't want any part of his royal life. She wanted intimacy and love, the kind of closeness she suspected Helen and Alain enjoyed, not a relationship carried out in the full glare of public scrutiny, where duty and responsibility came before everything else.

Her gaze automatically sought out Lorne, standing head and shoulders above the group who had claimed his attention. Tonight was a perfect example of the life he was expected to lead. Instead of enjoying a hard-earned break, he was spending his evening entertaining as befitted his position.

While sipping champagne, she watched him covertly, unwillingly impressed by how easily he moved from one group to another, exchanging a few words with each guest. She wondered how many of them caught the fine lines she noticed around his eyes and mouth. To her they spoke of the strain of rarely being off duty.

The champagne must be making her fanciful, she decided. Since when had Lorne de Marigny's state of mind concerned her? She wasn't about to get personally involved with him, so why should she care what demands royal life imposed on him? He had bonded her to him to teach her a lesson, not to keep her at his side. As soon as the two months of her sentence were up, he would probably put her on the first plane back to Australia without a second thought.

"I'm sure you mean well, but I only work for the prince," she assured Helen. She felt drawn to the older woman, but couldn't let the comment pass unchallenged.

Helen Pascale gave a knowing smile. "Funny, that's exactly what I used to tell myself about Alain."

Allie gave up. Helen was obviously a romantic, but she would find out the truth soon enough. In the meantime there was no reason they couldn't enjoy each other's company. Before long Allie had accepted Helen's pressing invitation to visit their villa, not far from the royal residence.

"Since Alain is often on call at the palace, we have a town house in Solano, as well, so you're welcome to visit us there," Helen insisted.

Since Helen was determined to see romance where none existed, Allie didn't point out that she didn't plan to return to the capital with the royal household. With luck her tenure would be up before the question arose. "I appreciate the invitation," she dissembled.

Helen's hands fluttered expressively, a habit she had evidently acquired locally. "It's hardly kindness, Allie. You're Alain's favorite patient at the moment. He would want me to take care of you."

"He's been kind to me, but I'm hardly his patient any longer," Allie said with a smile. "I was run-down when I arrived, and getting caught in a rip was the last straw, but I'm fully recovered now."

Helen regarded her critically. "You look a little pale to me, and far too thin." She hailed a passing waiter with a gesture and hovered over Allie until she ate another delicious morsel. "I'll have to make sure that slave driver, Lorne, doesn't work you too hard," she admonished.

Allie would hate Lorne to think she had complained to

his friends. "It's the opposite, in fact," she denied. "My duties as Nori's companion take up very little time. I feel almost guilty having so little to do."

"That's not what I hear from Alain. According to him, you spend far too much time shut away in your studio."

Allie gave a quick, rueful grin. "I suppose I do spend a lot of time painting, but it is the reason why I'm here. Working for the prince wasn't part of my original plans. Not that I don't enjoy looking after Nori," she added hastily.

"He is a sweet child, isn't he?" Helen agreed. "It's a shame that…"

Helen's voice trailed off, and Allie's curiosity stirred. "What is a shame?"

"Nothing really. I was only going to say that he seems a bit lonely."

Allie nodded agreement. "To me, too. Tonight I plan to ask Lorne to let me invite some other children to play with Nori."

Helen gave a concerned frown. "Don't be surprised if he's less than enthusiastic."

Allie waved away a waiter offering more food. "Why would he mind? I know he spends as much time with his son as he can, but as a teacher I feel a four-year-old needs children his own age as well as adult company."

"You don't know a lot about Lorne's marriage, do you?" Helen asked with seeming irrelevance.

"Only the few details he has told me himself."

Helen chewed her lower lip thoughtfully. "Then I'd better let him tell you more himself if he wants to, but don't be surprised if he's against inviting children to the villa. He isn't being difficult, it's just…"

Again that infuriating pause. Before Allie could urge the other woman to continue, the orchestra struck up a dance number. Lorne appeared at her elbow. "Will you do me the honor?"

Apprehension fluttered through Allie. The floor had cleared in anticipation of the dancing, and it was obvious that no one else could take to the floor until the prince did. She was conscious of every eye upon them. Making a scene would never do, and yet the last thing she wanted was to be taken in his arms in front of everyone.

"I'm not that great a dancer," she murmured for his ears alone.

"That makes two of us," he confided with a smile. "One of the advantages of my position is that no one dares to comment. Shall we?"

Dancing with him would provide the perfect opportunity to ask him about playmates for Nori, she told herself. Still she hesitated, suspecting that the pulse beating wildly in her throat signaled a response far more personal than concern for his child.

The suspicion became fact when he swept her into his arms, permitting no more discussion. Desire jolted through her, soul searing in its intensity, touching depths she had never suspected she possessed.

For the first few moments, they had the floor to themselves, but Allie was no longer conscious of the watching guests, only of the pressure of Lorne's hold on her, as if he would mold her to some heart's desire of his own.

His touch was as warm and firm as she had imagined while dressing earlier, and almost of their own accord her feet followed his lead. He had been honest with her. He wasn't a skilled dancer, but he moved with a natural grace that more than compensated for any lack of technical ability. For her part she had never danced so lightly or easily in her life.

"Enjoying the party?" he asked softly.

She nodded, too overwhelmed by his nearness to trust her voice.

"You seem to have made a friend of Helen Pascale."

Safe ground at last. "The feeling's mutual. She's very easy to like."

"Unlike your employer," he commented with uncanny insight.

She forced her head up, startled by the brilliance of his eyes upon her but resisting the compulsion to look away. She couldn't conceive of a feeling as feeble as mere liking toward Lorne. As a man of passion he demanded passionate responses, like hate or—no, she wouldn't permit herself to think it. "I thought you decreed we're equals tonight," she said, her thoughts reflected in a breathlessness she hoped he would blame on the dancing.

He inclined his head slowly, his eyes thoughtful. "As an equal, then, tell me what is in your thoughts."

She had asked for this. She drew a shaky breath, wishing the music would end so she could move away from his compelling presence, not because she didn't enjoy it but because she feared enjoying it too much. Sharing this thought with him was unthinkable so she substituted, "I was thinking how good it feels to be a free woman again, for one night at least."

He studied her keenly. "Freedom is important to you, isn't it, Alison?"

Thinking of the years when living her own life, free of the demands of her family, had been an impossible dream, she nodded. It was the cruelest irony that in bonding her to him, Lorne had chosen the one punishment she would find hardest to tolerate. She felt like a caged bird who had been allowed to fly a couple of circuits around a room, only to be entrapped again.

His brows drew together. "I suppose when you're used

to pleasing yourself it is difficult to be bound by someone else's rules.''

It was so unfair and far from the truth that anger surged through her. She felt an irrational urge to hurt him as badly as his words had injured her. ''Are you referring to me or your marriage?''

Her wild shot had hit home, she saw from the dark glitter in his eyes. His hold on her became punishing. She would probably have a bruise on her shoulder tomorrow from the feel of his fingers gripping her delicate skin. She glanced at his hand, and he seemed to become aware of what he was doing, his hold slackening slightly. But he didn't release her. ''Perhaps I was referring to both, since rebellion is evidently a part of your national character.''

''Comes from having a convict past,'' she muttered. She was horrified at herself for striking such a low blow, but she disliked being categorized with his late wife as an irresponsible rebel. ''We tend to rebel against any authority when it's unjustly applied.''

''So I'm keeping you here unjustly, is that it?''

She stuck out her chin. ''Since you asked, yes. What did I do that was so terrible? Women have been slapping men's faces since the dawn of time.''

''Perhaps, but not a monarch's,'' he put in silkily.

She seized her opportunity. ''In other words we are equals, but if you're royal, you're more equal than others.''

The music ended, catching her unawares. Lorne gave a courtly half bow, but his expression was thunderous. ''I gather your problem is with me as a ruler, rather than as a man?''

Without answering she glared back at him but let him take her elbow and steer her to the fringe of the dance floor, close to one of the sets of French doors leading to the terrace. She welcomed the feel of the cool, evening breeze on her heated cheeks, hating to think Lorne could be right.

Could she deal with him more readily as a man than as a prince?

The question was academic, anyway, she assured herself, darting a furious look at him. After she left Carramer, she wouldn't see him again in any guise, man or prince. "Is my attitude so surprising?" she demanded. "The prince is the one who keeps throwing his weight around. I've hardly had a chance to meet the man."

"If things had been different, would you like to?"

Her heart turned over. If Lorne had been an ordinary man instead of a prince, who knew where their relationship might have led? But he *was* a prince so it was wishing for the impossible. "Things can't be different, so what's the point in discussing it?" She felt overheated suddenly and a little faint...from the dancing and the crowd, she assumed.

He took in her distress at a glance and summoned a waiter to bring her water in a crystal goblet. "Let us go outside, the evening air will revive you," he suggested.

The last thing she wanted was to be alone with him on the terrace, although she had fantasized about it earlier in the evening. "I'm fine," she insisted, finishing the water.

He took the goblet from her and set it down. "Must you argue every edict I issue, even those with your good in mind?"

"You could try asking me instead of issuing edicts."

His eyebrow lifted sardonically, and a breath escaped as a slight sigh. "Alison, will you join me outside for a moment?"

It was a victory of sorts, but it felt more like a trap. There was only one possible response. "Yes."

She knew it was a mistake as soon as he steered her onto the terrace. Outside the air was fragrant with the blossoms of a thousand tropical flowers and as intoxicating as wine.

Music spilled through the open doors, but the voices of the party guests were muted out here.

Only a handful of people had wandered outside, most preferring to join the dancing inside. Lorne led her between the flaming torches until they were swallowed up by the darkness. "Feeling better now?" he asked, his voice a velvet caress in the night.

"Yes, thank you." She no longer felt faint, if that was what he meant. Instead her pulses had set up a much more disturbing beat. Did he have to stand so close to her? It made thinking difficult and breathing even more of a challenge.

She told herself it was the strangeness of having someone so concerned for her welfare. She was more accustomed to looking after others than to having someone fuss over her. If he hadn't been the prince...

"There's no need to neglect your guests on my account," she insisted.

Her eyes had adjusted to the darkness, and she saw him glance toward the brightness where the party was in full swing. "Do they look neglected to you?"

"No, but they'll wonder what we're doing out here." She thought of the mothers who had brought their daughters along, obviously hoping to catch the prince's eye.

He gave a soft chuckle, and she saw that she had been read like a book. "If you mean those two dragons I saw glaring at you earlier, it will do them good to wonder. Maybe they'll get the message that if I choose another bride, it will be in my own way and time."

Allie felt hugely let down. Although she hadn't wanted Lorne's romantic attention in the velvet darkness, she was surprised how much it hurt to be relegated to the role of smokescreen, keeping the prince out of the clutches of the matchmaking matrons.

Disappointment sharpened her tone. "While we're alone,

there is something I want to discuss with you. It's about Nori."

She recaptured his attention instantly, but there was no intimacy in it. "Is something wrong?"

"Haven't you noticed how lonely he is?"

There was a long pause. "He's hardly lonely. I spend every free hour I have with him. His nanny takes good care of his personal needs, and you provide the companionship he requires the rest of the time."

"I wasn't accusing you of neglecting him," she said quickly, stung by the censure in his voice. "Considering your other responsibilities, you spend more time with him than most fathers."

"I'm glad I have your approval," he said dryly, "although I wasn't aware that I needed it."

He was pulling rank again, she noted despairingly. "Look, I thought you said we're equals tonight. I should be free to speak my mind, right?"

He made a sound of disapproval. "Is there any force on earth capable of stopping you?"

There was so much pain in his voice that she felt stunned. "I'm not Chandra," she said softly.

He pulled in a sharp breath. "I'm well aware of the fact, but it's obvious that you have many traits in common."

"If you stifled her opinions as frequently as you do mine, no wonder it didn't work out," she said, his coldness making her reckless. She didn't like being tarred with the same brush as his late wife.

"Have you quite finished?"

His arctic tone should have warned her, but she was too worked up to retreat now. "No, I haven't. Nori is only four years old. He's wiser than most toddlers his age, but he's still a baby and he needs the company of other children."

There, she'd said it. She stood silent, waiting for the storm to break. It wasn't long in coming. "I'm sure Nori's nanny and probably others have told you that I don't want other children underfoot," he said harshly. "The subject is closed."

"It can't be." As he started to turn away, she put a hand on his arm, meaning only to regain his attention. She did but in a way that shocked her with its intensity. As soon as her fingers closed around his arm, she felt fire start at her fingertips and race all the way along her nerves, almost making her pull away in raw panic. He loomed over her, his eyes seeming to blaze in the reflected torchlight.

To her astonishment she found she ached to touch him more intimately, to have him touch her the same way. He didn't even like her. With her outspoken Australian ways she reminded him too much of his disastrous marriage. Yet she found herself wanting him to look at her with approval, instead of glowering at her out of the darkness. What was going on here?

"I will overlook your outburst because you have Nori's best interests at heart," he said tautly, "but he is my son and I know what is best for him."

She had come too far to back down now, whatever the consequences, although she shuddered to think what they might be. "Are you a teacher? I am. I know about early childhood development, and you're in danger of stunting Nori's."

It was a low blow and she regretted it as soon as she saw pain cloud his expression, but she plunged on. "Laura Myss told me next Monday is Journey Day, a holiday dedicated to travelers and children setting out on their life's journey. She says traditionally the children receive gifts of books and toy boats or go to parties or on special excursions. It sounds like the perfect occasion for Nori to meet some of the local children. Can't we at least invite some of them to a Journey Day party?"

He looked surprised that she was aware of the custom

but shook his head. "Plan some other Journey Day cele-
bration, but not that." And he went back inside, leaving
her standing fuming on the terrace.

So that was that. He hadn't given her a chance to use
any of her carefully developed reasoning, based on her
teaching experience. She would have believed he was simply pulling royal rank again if not for the pain she had
glimpsed in his expression. No, there was more going on
here than Lorne's ego.

He was a haunted man, and every instinct urged her to
bring him what comfort she could. At some level she knew
her feelings went deeper than simple compassion, but how
deep? And where could they possibly lead?

She tried telling herself that Nori was the reason she
cared so much. The little boy had carved a large place in
her heart in a short time. But a much larger space was in
danger of being filled by his charismatic father.

No! The word screamed through her mind. Lorne was a
prince with a kingdom to run and little room in his life for
anything else. His disastrous marriage was proof of what
his demanding lifestyle could do to a relationship.

All the same he was attracted to her, she knew, and pity
help her, the feeling was mutual. He was the most charming, sexy and exciting man she had ever met. From what
she had seen, his staff loved him and his people worshiped
him. But he was like a man with a huge ready-made family
any woman would be taking on if she got involved with
him.

When had she started to imagine sharing his life? she
wondered. With a man who was never off duty, where
would be the private moments, the intimacy and, yes, the
freedom to live their own life? Nonexistent, that's where,
she told herself glumly. It was just as well to face it before
she did anything stupid like fall in love with Lorne.

Chapter Nine

The urge to fling himself out of the room and go after Alison and his son was very strong, but years of royal training kept Lorne at his desk, trying not to let his shock show in his body. "She has taken my son where?"

Even the normally irascible Dr. Pascale looked uncomfortable, well aware of being the bearer of unwelcome news. "It seems she and Laura Myss have taken Nori to visit a kindergarten in Allora operated by Laura's sister."

"Alone?" Lorne couldn't believe even Alison would be so stupid.

The doctor shook his head. "They have the usual contingent of minders who all believe, as I did, that you approved of the trip."

Lorne's lowered brows told their own story. "Now you know better." He drummed his fingers against the leather desktop. "I told her I didn't want other children around."

Crossing his arms over his chest, the doctor watched Lorne in concern. "I think what we have here is a misunderstanding. You told Allie not to invite the children to the villa, but you didn't tell her not to take Nori to them, right?''

"Semantics. Playing with words." Lorne spat the phrase out, but the doctor knew him too well to be cowed by the display of temper.

"I'm right, aren't I?"

Lorne took a deep breath and spared his friend a withering look. "Don't you ever get tired of being right?"

"Nope. It's one of the few compensations I get out of working for you."

Lorne scowled. "There must be other doctors in this kingdom prepared to respect the crown, who would jump at the chance of a royal appointment."

Alain Pascale looked unperturbed. "Probably, but they don't play a mean game of chess like I do."

Lorne refused to continue the old altercation. He'd threatened to dismiss Alain more times than he could remember, but they both knew it would never happen. Lorne needed the older man's wisdom and frankness, perhaps more than he needed his medical advice.

"All the same, I can't let Alison do as she pleases where Nori is concerned," he stated flatly. He wasn't sure which of her actions had angered him more—her taking his son away without his permission, or the clever way she had twisted his words when his meaning had been perfectly clear. She was the most infuriating woman he had ever encountered.

She was also the most beautiful and resourceful, he conceded to himself. Few women of his acquaintance would have defied him so openly. Another reason he couldn't allow her to get away with it.

"Have them brought back immediately," he ordered. "I want to see Alison the moment she returns."

Alain's eyebrows lifted quizzically. "Are you sure it's wise to take Nori away so abruptly? Between his nanny, his guards and Alison herself, he's as safe as he would be under your roof and he's probably having the time of his life."

Lorne sighed deeply, afraid that the doctor was right— again. He said so, adding, "Being a competent chess player doesn't give you limitless immunity."

The doctor looked affronted. "Competent? Who won the last three games?" Then he saw the strain of the situation etched on Lorne's features and relented. "This isn't only about Alison, is it? It's the idea of Nori among the other children that bothers you."

Lorne shot him a barbed look almost anyone else would have heeded. "Enough, Alain."

The doctor wasn't just anyone. Long ago he had appointed himself Lorne's mentor, counselor and conscience when needed. It was needed now. "Even your royal powers can't change the past, Lorne. Isn't it time you accepted what happened, for Nori's sake if not for your own?"

The use of his first name told Lorne the lecture was far from over. It was the doctor's way of reminding the prince that he got out of bed one leg at a time in the morning, just like everyone else in the kingdom.

Usually Lorne appreciated the doctor's reasoning if not his methods but today he was too aggravated by Alison's behavior to welcome the counsel, however sound or well-meant.

He raked his fingers through his hair. "This is hardly the right time, Doctor."

The title was another signal between them that Lorne was not in the mood for fatherly advice. The doctor took as much notice of it as he usually did. "All the schools are having celebrations today in preparation for the Journey Day holiday. Allie probably thought she was doing the right thing letting Nori be a part of it. It's not as if she's kidnapped him."

Lorne's head came up. "She may as well have done. Why didn't someone check with me before letting her take him to visit this…kindergarten, wherever it is?"

"It's a couple of miles along the coast toward Allora," the doctor said in a long-suffering tone. "It has an excellent reputation, and the children who attend come from good families—I checked. As for why she didn't tell you in advance, have you looked in a mirror lately?"

Lorne didn't need a mirror. His pounding pulse was proof enough of his furious state of mind. "I have a right to be angry," he said forcefully. "You say it's time I accepted what happened, but it's tough to do when the loss involves not only your wife but the twin babies you didn't even know she was carrying."

The doctor's craggy features softened. "I agree it was a rough way to find out that your wife was pregnant, after she died."

"Every time I see a group of laughing, playing children I think of those babies, the brother and sister Nori should have had," Lorne went on, his voice raw. "Is it any wonder I don't want to be reminded of what could have been? When her car went over the cliff, Chandra condemned my son to be an only child."

"She wasn't the only one," the doctor said so softly that he could have been speaking to himself.

A cold breath touched Lorne. "Explain yourself."

"Do I need to? We both know what you lost that day was a marriage, not a love affair. The love died long before."

Lorne felt as if he could break something. Or someone. "Your point, Doctor?"

"If anyone's condemning Nori to be an only child now, it's his father. You're young, virile and quite possibly halfway in love already, but you won't allow yourself to accept that, either."

Lorne lowered his brows, telling himself that the doctor couldn't be more wrong. "So you're a mind reader now as well as a medical doctor?"

His friend shrugged. "Sometimes doctors have to be both. Allie is the key to all this, isn't she? You're not only mad at her for taking Nori away without your permission. You're mad at her because she has a stiff neck you can't bend. And you very much want to."

"I don't love Alison Carter."

Ignoring the steel in Lorne's voice, the doctor worried at the point like a terrier with a bone. "You don't or you won't? Is it because she's Australian like Chandra or because she's a woman, ditto?"

"You were lucky with your marriage," Lorne said slowly. "How would you have felt if things between you and Helen had been different, if she had loved not you but your position and not your country but the leaving of it?"

The doctor looked thoughtful. "I suppose I'd have felt much as you do, betrayed, a bit gun-shy. But I would hope if someone as special as Allie came my way, I'd be able to get over those feelings and start living again, for my son if not for myself."

Lorne's breath hissed out in frustration. "We're back to Alison again. Has it occurred to you that I might prefer a woman who actually likes me?"

The doctor gave him a startled look. "What makes you think she doesn't like you?"

Lorne spreads his hands wide. "She argues every point, challenges me at every turn. Today is only the latest example of her waywardness."

The doctor grinned. "Sounds like love to me. At least life with her would never be dull."

"You are mistaking wildness for passion," the prince said. He didn't add that he had experienced Alison's passion when he kissed her and again when he held her as they danced. Admitting it would only fuel Alain's crazy notion that anything lasting could come of a relationship with her.

It wasn't as if she wanted anything to do with him. Not by a word or gesture had she suggested that she felt anything for him, other than disdain for his position. Physical attraction was another matter.

Lorne couldn't deny that he wanted her more than he had ever wanted any woman. She wanted him, too, he would swear. A tremor gripped him as he remembered the pliant feel of her in his arms and the response he had evoked from her mouth.

She had aroused a need in him like the fiercest kind of hunger, and her reactions told him she felt the same. She had tried to rebel against it, but it was too strong to conceal from him entirely. The temptation to push beyond the boundaries of her resistance to the Heaven he wanted her to know had been almost irresistible. White heat pulsed through him at the very thought. He fought it. One marriage where the only shared pleasures were physical ones was quite enough. He wanted much more before he was prepared to risk committing himself again.

Then there were her paintings, a truer measure of Alison's opinion of Lorne than her physical reactions, he thought. When Alison wasn't with Nori or Lorne himself, she spent every spare minute painting. Visiting the studio unannounced, he had caught her erasing a portrait, but enough of it remained for Lorne to recognize his own likeness.

Had she scrubbed it out in a fit of antipathy toward him? It seemed likely. Her paintings of Nori were so tender and beautiful that Lorne's heart had constricted at the sight of them. There was no such tenderness in the destroyed portrait of Lorne himself.

"You're imagining things, Doctor," he said flatly.

"Am I imagining that absurd bond you slapped on her?"

Before Lorne could reply, Alain plunged on, "It's the talk of the household by now. What did she do to deserve such a punishment? No one's used it in this country in years."

"What she did and how I choose to respond is my affair," Lorne said with all the regal authority he could muster. He wasn't about to admit acting in the heat of the moment or how much he regretted it now. What was done was done.

"The bond is only for two months, and she has already served half of it. In any case, today's episode shows how ready she is to flout Carramer law. Until the bond is served, she has no legal right to leave the home of her bond master without permission, but it doesn't seem to have stopped her."

"Maybe you didn't make the conditions clear enough," the doctor said.

"I did. She has about as much regard for my position as...as you have."

Ignoring the slur, the doctor chuckled. "And you wonder why she doesn't fall all over you. My advice is to change tactics. Treat her like a lady you could care for instead of a bonded servant and I'll bet things improve between you."

The doctor was assuming Lorne wanted them to, he thought sourly. Even if he did, Alison obviously didn't. "Thank you for the advice, Doctor," he said stiffly, his tone rejecting it out of hand. "You may see yourself out."

The doctor lifted his hands in mock surrender. "As Your Highness wishes. All the same, I wish you'd think about it before Allie gets back."

Lorne's mouth twisted into a humorless smile. "I shall give your advice all the consideration it deserves."

It had been such a wonderful morning that Allie had managed to push the likely consequences of her action to the back of her mind. As the limousine carried them back to the villa, the enormity of what she had done weighed heavily on her. Seeing Nori, tired but happy, his small body curled against her as he dozed, she knew it would be worth whatever price Lorne exacted from her.

"The little prince enjoyed his first experience of school," Laura Myss murmured as if reading Allie's thoughts.

Allie nodded. "It was a great experience for me, too. Your sister is a wonderful teacher. Using hand puppets to explain the origins of Journey Day really made the story come alive, especially when she let each child work one of the puppets."

Laura smiled. "Naturally, Nori had to play the part of the ancient ruler whose journey united the islands of Carramer long ago. The way he threw himself into the role, one would think he'd rather be a tyrant of old than a benevolent prince like his father."

Lorne had shown little benevolence toward Allie, but she kept the thought to herself. "Nori's still sorting out his role," she said. "Being around other children will help him to keep his feet on the ground."

The little boy made a sleepy sound of protest. "My feet wasn't on the ground when we played the jumping game. It was fun."

Hiding her smile, Allie gave him a hug. "I'm glad you think so."

Then Nori gazed up at her solemnly. "I'm glad, too. Even if the naughty children wouldn't stop calling me Nori."

Baffled, Allie glanced at Laura but the nanny looked equally bewildered. "What's wrong with them calling you by your name?"

Nori puffed out his small chest. "They have to call me Your Highness. They're naughty children, 'cause they laughed when I ordered them to."

It was all Allie could do not to laugh herself. She buried her reaction in a cough. "They want to be your friends. Friends call each other by their names, not their titles."

Nori digested this in silence, then said, "I s'pose it's all right then. Can we go and see my friends again tomorrow?"

Allie bit her lower lip. "I don't know, sweetheart. It's up to your father." She was already fairly sure how he would greet such a request.

"I'm surprised the prince permitted this visit," Laura mused, evidently sharing Allie's doubts.

Allie felt herself coloring. "He didn't exactly permit it. He just didn't say I couldn't take Nori to the school."

The nanny clutched a hand to her mouth. "You mean he doesn't know? Oh, Allie, we will be in terrible trouble when he finds out."

Ice slid along Allie's veins, but she smiled defiantly. "Not we...me. I'll make sure the prince knows that it was my idea. It's the truth, after all."

Laura's chin came up. "We are friends, too. I will say it was also my doing."

Touched more than she could put into words, Allie rested a hand on top of Laura's. "Thanks, but I can't allow it. You have to live here after I return to Australia." From the sound of things it could be sooner than expected, and a pang shot through Allie at the thought.

She would miss Carramer. In the past few weeks she had come to love the generous, openhearted people and the gentle island lifestyle. She had even adjusted to the concept of *Carramer time* meaning nothing was ever hurried or pressured. If something wasn't done today, it would be done tomorrow or the next day. Stress was almost unheard of, except among the visitors who insisted on trying to see every inch of the islands in a few days.

When had she stopped thinking of herself as a visitor?

she wondered in some consternation. It had happened so gradually that she couldn't pinpoint the change. Yet at some stage she had started to feel as if she belonged here, when the opposite was true, as she feared she was about to find out.

The moment the limousine and its escort arrived at the summer palace, an aide delivered Lorne's summons to Allie. Laura looked alarmed, but Allie masked her trepidation with a reassuring smile.

"Take Nori back to the nursery. I'll be fine." Inwardly she wondered for how long. How did Carramer law view the breaking of a personal bond? She hoped it qualified as a misdemeanor rather than a capital offense.

That was a forlorn hope, she thought when she saw Lorne's expression. The prince looked as angry as she had ever seen him and then some, and her heart sank. She had expected him to be furious with her but hadn't expected it to hurt quite this much.

A door closed behind the aide, leaving her alone with the prince. She squared her shoulders. "I can explain everything."

Lorne's jaw was set hard. "Don't you mean try to justify your high-handed behavior? Don't bother. I could put the breaking of your bond down to ignorance of our laws, but there can be no justification for taking my son away against my express wishes."

Her temper flared. "Aren't you exaggerating a bit, Your Highness?" Her use of his title sounded anything but deferential, but it was right in line with her mood. "All I did was take Nori on a Journey Day outing that you hadn't expressly forbidden. He had a wonderful time, thank you for asking."

Lorne's fist crashed against the desk, and she jumped. "You are the most insolent—"

"Australian?" she supplied helpfully, concealing her

alarm. Inwardly she was horrified at herself. Facing the firing squad was one thing, but helping to load the rifles quite another. Somehow Lorne managed to provoke her into rebellious actions.

What had happened to Allie Carter of the overdeveloped sense of responsibility? Around Lorne that Allie was replaced by a woman whose blood heated and temper soared, along with her heart and pulse rate, driving her to reckless extremes. She hated the effect he had on her, but couldn't seem to control it.

"Give me a good reason why I shouldn't have you locked up to serve out the rest of your bond," Lorne demanded, sounding drained.

She pushed away the compassion his tone wanted to kindle in her and went for broke. "Give *me* a good reason why you don't want other children around, when they're exactly what your little boy needs."

He came around his desk like a bullet out of a gun, and she resisted the urge to step back from the ferocity she read in his eyes. His hands clamped around her upper arms, and she no longer had a choice but to meet his unrelenting gaze. "You want a good reason? Very well. When my wife died, she was pregnant with twins, a girl and a boy. Whenever I hear children laughing, I'm reminded that my babies never had a chance to live."

It was so unexpected that she sagged in his grasp. She had never dreamed that his loss had been so great. Seeing Nori with other children must be torture for him, reminding him of what should have been. "Oh, Lorne, if I'd had any idea, I never would have insisted on taking Nori to the school."

"Oddly enough, I believe you," he said, sounding hoarse. "Your methods are intolerable, but I'm sure you had my son's best interests at heart."

"You must believe I did." Her voice came out as a

fervent whisper. It didn't change her belief that Nori needed playmates of his own age, but Lorne's feelings mattered to her, too. She was surprised how much.

The silence lengthened, deepened, and she became very much aware of being in his arms. She tensed, waiting for him to break the spell, move away, prescribe a new punishment for her, anything but what he did next.

Without warning he raised one hand to caress her neck while pulling her roughly against him with the other. The hard bone of his hip grazed hers as he turned her until her softness met the unmistakable fullness of his arousal. "Allie." His voice was a harsh baritone.

He bent his head and kissed her just as she registered that he had used her nickname for the first time. Astonishment drove her lips apart, and he took full advantage of it to deepen the kiss.

At the sinuous touch of his tongue against her sensitive palate, she felt dizzy from the sensory onslaught. Her heart started to trip-hammer so loudly that it was a wonder he didn't hear it.

Her fingers flexed with the urge to touch him. She wanted to wind her hands around his neck and give herself fully to the sensations swirling through her. Given who and what he was, though, she couldn't risk it.

She hadn't realized she had arched against him until she felt the fierce pounding of his heart keeping time with hers. He had threatened to imprison her, but what was this, if not imprisonment of the sweetest, most dangerous kind?

When had she developed a taste for forbidden fruit? she wondered in a kind of sensual haze. Lorne was everything she shouldn't want in a man. Belonging so completely to his people, how could he ever belong to one woman? The debacle of his marriage proved how impossible it was. The thought should have stemmed the tide of longing flooding her being, but it only served to heighten her excitement.

When Lorne bent her back against his desk and leaned over her, supporting his weight on his arms, she felt the room start to spin. Everything spiraled in until he filled her field of vision. This might be a mistake but she didn't want it to end.

Her breathing faltered as he eased her peasant blouse off her shoulders and teased her sun-kissed skin with his teeth. Her mouth dried, and liquid fire raced through her. Her fingers raked his shoulders, pulling him against her, wanting him in spite of the reasons why she shouldn't.

The ancients of Carramer had called it *woman-fever,* and it sang in Lorne's veins now as he leaned over Allie. His breathing was ragged and his control hung by a thread. He wanted to possess her, but more, he wanted to wake up beside her every morning and drive the heaviness of sleep from her eyes with his passion.

"Oh, Lorne."

Like an arrow, her husky voice pierced his desire-fogged thoughts, and he froze, gripped by self-reproach. The feeling was barely enough to stop him. Her long hair flowed across his desk and her full lips were half-open in response to his kisses. Her filmy blouse rode low on her shoulders and he was horrified to see the marks of his mouth marring their golden perfection.

What was he doing? He was as near as he had ever come to violating his own laws. In placing Allie under bond, he was legally bound to protect her even from himself. He could correct, advise, punish if necessary, but never take advantage of her while she was bonded to him.

It took all of his resolve to lever himself away from her and help her to straighten up. The puzzled hurt in her expression tore at him. He wanted to kiss it away, but he resisted the urge, knowing where it had to lead. The thought made him turn away, and even that was a mistake, as the small sounds of Allie adjusting her clothing quickened his desire again.

"What's wrong, Lorne?" she asked in a small voice.

He winced at her injured tone. "Nothing's wrong," he said, although every aching muscle in his body screamed a contradiction. "The bond requires you to obey me, but not to that extent. You may go."

"Just like that?"

He clenched his fists. If she didn't leave quickly, he wouldn't be able to let her go at all.

Allie looked at Lorne's rigid back, bewildered by the abrupt change. She told herself to be grateful for his restraint, but with desire pulsing through her veins, gratitude was the last thing she felt.

His message was clear enough. He didn't want her in any way, not even physically, and if she had any sense, she would leave as ordered. Too bad taking orders had never been her strong suit. "There's more, isn't there, Lorne? Something you aren't telling me?"

He flung himself around, his eyes blazing. "If you must know, the bond imposes obligations on both of us."

Her eyes widened. "Obligations like not sleeping with someone who's bonded to you?" He nodded. Thinking of how close he had come to breaking the covenant, she began to understand. "You could unbond me," she offered, astonishing herself.

"I could but I won't," he said flatly. Right now the bond was the only thing protecting her from him.

He didn't want to release her, she accepted with a heavy heart, seeing only that she had offered him a solution and he hadn't taken it. What had she expected? Eager acceptance and a declaration of love? What would she have done then? Married him and become his princess?

Be real, she told herself. After his disastrous marriage, he wasn't about to propose to someone so like his late wife.

Was he thinking of his wife when he kissed Allie? Had she stirred memories by taking Nori away? Confused and hurt, she said, "May I go now, Your Highness?"

His head inclined regally. "Yes." He fiddled with the gold pen set on his desk. "There is one more thing. Your idea of a Journey Day treat for Nori has inspired me. I shall take him to Isle des Anges to swim with the dolphins. You will accompany us."

After what had happened, going anywhere with him was unwise, but she was learning. "As you wish, Your Highness."

He lifted an eyebrow in sardonic comment. "Surrender, Allie?"

She said nothing but he was sure he heard her mutter as she went out, "In a pig's eye."

"I'll show him surrender," Allie muttered furiously to herself as she slammed into the studio. Laura had fed Nori and tucked him into bed for a nap, so Allie was off duty for the afternoon. Frustration whirled through her, and she knew exactly how to assuage it.

Three hours later she dashed a hand across her damp forehead, blotting paint and perspiration out of her eyes. The portrait of Lorne, painted at white heat, was finished.

Working from a memory she hadn't consciously captured, she had clothed him in the costume of his ancestor, the Prince Jacques de Ville de Marigny. Jacques had been the first reigning monarch to journey around all of Carramer's islands, unifying them for the first time in their history. His voyage was commemorated throughout the kingdom as Journey Day.

Inspired by a woodcut the teacher at the kindergarten had shown to the children, Allie had painted Lorne wearing pants of some soft, kidlike material that hugged the powerful contours of his legs. His magnificent chest was bare but for a jerkin of similar material laced across his taut muscles. Over his shoulders he wore a long, feathered cloak, fastened at the front by a jeweled emblem of office.

With his feet apart and hands on hips he stood on a clifftop, the ocean seething at his feet as if paying homage. His brooding gaze swept over a hazy landscape as if he ruled not only the land and the sea but the vast sky above.

His kisses, so exciting until they were abruptly withdrawn, had driven her to the canvas, she admitted to herself. She had worked in a frenzy, dissipating her frustration in an activity as physically demanding as his lovemaking would have been. She knew a sense of release now it was done, but there the resemblance ended. The ache of loneliness remained. However lifelike it was—and she had to admit it was the best thing she had ever done—no painted man could love her, any more than it seemed the real one wanted to do.

She tossed her brush into the muddle of paint and rags, lacking the strength to tidy up. As an afterthought she turned the easel so that Lorne's portrait faced a wall. She propped a recent study of Nori against the easel in case the prince thought to wonder what she'd been doing. Too much raw emotion had gone into the portrait for her to want Lorne to see it and question her feelings when she didn't understand them herself.

She wished he hadn't insisted she accompany him and Nori to the nearby island governed by his brother, Prince Michel. It smacked too much of intruding on a family occasion. There would be minders, of course. They shadowed the royal family everywhere outside the villa walls. Normally she found their presence nerve-wracking but this time she knew she would be far more tense if she and Lorne made the trip by themselves.

Her nerves fluttered a protest as she remembered the hard warmth of his mouth against hers. Liquid heat suffused her.

She didn't want him to kiss her again, while she ran her fingers through the silken strands of his hair and along the hard planes of his back. Or to have him crush her against him, the contact more arousing than anything she had ever known.

She didn't want any of it. He didn't love her and certainly didn't want a repeat of his marriage. She didn't want to love a man so alien to everything she knew that they might as well be from different planets. It couldn't possibly work. Fear sparked through her. And something else. A need so fierce that she moaned aloud and crossed her arms over her body to fight it.

She knew what it was. It was the aching need to be loved. She could have killed Lorne for making her see how much she needed it. She had been doing well enough on her own, managing her life as she had managed her mother's and sister's, afraid to let go of the reins in case there was no one else to pick them up.

Afraid.

The word hung in her mind, stark and terrifying. With his kisses Lorne had made her face what she had hidden from herself for so long. She was afraid of loving and losing. Pity help her, she was afraid of loving and losing *him.*

Chapter Ten

Journey Day was a public holiday in Carramer. From the royal helicopter she looked down on a flotilla of small craft dotting the strait between the main island of Celeste and Isle des Anges. "It looks like half of Carramer is out on the water," she said to Nori. The child could hardly contain his excitement, both at the novelty of the helicopter ride and at the adventure ahead.

"Are we really going to swim with dolphins?" he asked Allie.

Lorne met her questioning glance. "We'll swim where they are usually found, *coquine*. It's up to the dolphins whether they want to swim with us."

"They'll come if you tell them who I am," Nori said with such confidence that Allie was forced to laugh.

"They probably will." Love for the little boy tugged at her, his curious mixture of regal arrogance and baby charm threatening to melt her heart. What she wouldn't give to be a mother to him and to give him the brothers and sisters he deserved.

Her heart almost stopped as she considered what it would take to fulfill the wish. She looked at Lorne through a screen of lashes and was startled to find him studying her speculatively. He couldn't possibly have guessed what she was thinking. All the same she felt a blush starting and looked quickly away.

Through the Plexiglas she saw Isle des Anges approaching rapidly and immediately understood how it came by its name. From the air its shape, like an angel's wings, could be seen clearly. As they came in to land she glimpsed white sand beaches fringing stands of tropical rainforest. Native orchids, vines and fern trees threatened to spill over onto the helipad, and a flock of sulphur-colored parrots rose screeching from the pad as they approached.

She had thought the main island was beautiful, but Isle des Anges took her breath away. It was a magical, romantic place, possibly the last place on earth she should be with Lorne.

A convoy of luxurious off-road vehicles met them at the airstrip, and they were driven to the palace at Aviso, where Lorne's brother, Michel, had his seat of government. Nori bounced up and down in the car, his eyes round. "Will Uncle Michel be waiting for us?"

"Of course," Lorne said with a fond laugh. "Sit still, *coquine,* or you'll frighten away the dolphins."

Nori instantly made himself as small as possible, peering over the edge of the car window as if the dolphins could observe his every move. "Do you think they saw me?" he asked Allie.

She masked her smile. "You stopped fidgeting just in time."

The palace came into sight, and the dolphins were forgotten for the moment as Nori craned for a glimpse of his uncle. Allie was also curious to meet Lorne's younger brother, wondering whether she would gain any new insights into Lorne's character through his family.

The palace was a sprawling coral-colored building with carved columns supporting a porte cochere in the front where their convoy pulled up. Honey eaters swooped and dived beneath the porte cochere, unafraid of the new arrivals.

She stepped out of the car into warm, orchid-scented air just as a tall, well-built man came down the steps, taking them two at a time. Michel de Marigny, Allie guessed. He looked at most two years younger than Lorne, with the same elegant features, prominent cheekbones and strong jaw. His shoulders were almost sinfully wide under a monogrammed chocolate polo shirt tucked into butter-colored pants.

Allie frowned. With everything monogrammed, the brothers would have a hard time losing anything, although Michel's confident air suggested he seldom lost much anyway, not games, battles or love matches.

Ran in the family, she thought, her gaze drifting back to Lorne as the brothers greeted each other. When Lorne introduced Allie, Michel appraised her speculatively, but Lorne didn't elaborate. She wondered if Lorne made a habit of bringing minor staff members to family gatherings. Nori's nanny hadn't been invited.

Their escort fanned out around the grounds as Michel hoisted Nori onto his shoulders and led the way inside. "How's my favorite nephew?" He seemed comfortable around the little boy, and she wondered if he had any children of his own. If so, she saw no signs of them.

While they exchanged news, she made herself useful pouring the tea that had been set out. Lorne gave her an appreciative smile when she handed him a cup but took no more notice of her than he did of the other servants coming and going.

Annoyance flashed through her. What had she expected? Champagne and roses? She knew he regretted the shared moment of passion, but it hurt to find herself back in her slot, invisible except when she was waiting on him. She hid her anger. Letting him see how much his neglect bothered her would be far too revealing.

She forced her attention back to the brothers. "The yacht is ready, but I won't be joining you aboard," Michel was saying.

Lorne frowned. "Why not?"

"Would you believe that I have to take care of an affair of state?" Michel spoke lightly but she detected his faint undercurrent of resentment at being questioned.

She saw Lorne's mouth tighten. "Affair, perhaps. Of state, I doubt it. Have I met the woman who's keeping you from a family occasion?"

Michel shifted impatiently. "I don't believe so. I've only started seeing her recently."

Lorne sighed. "Another new one. When are you going to start behaving as befits your position, Michel?"

A glint of annoyance lit his brother's gaze but it was quickly masked. "Surely it's too fine a day for this discussion?"

Lorne looked as if he wanted to say more but seemed to become aware of Allie's presence at last. "I agree for now, but consider it a postponement. Even a prince can't evade responsibility forever."

So much for a family and children, Allie thought. Evidently playing the field also ran in the de Marigny family.

Moored at a marina in nearby Turtle Bay, Michel's yacht turned out to be a sleek sixty-foot ketch with a swimming platform at the back and every possible luxury inside. A glass of champagne welcomed them aboard, with orange juice for Nori.

So smooth was their departure that she hardly noticed

they were moving until she glimpsed the island falling rapidly astern. Most of their minders had peeled off at the jetty, she noticed. Presumably they were aboard the second vessel that shadowed them at a discreet distance. She had counted on the security team being aboard to provide a buffer between herself and Lorne. The yacht crew were practically invisible. Apart from Nori, she and Lorne could have been alone.

Changing into a swimsuit seemed like the height of folly, but Allie could think of no way around it. She couldn't supervise Nori from the saloon and she refused to let her feelings for Lorne prevent her from taking proper care of the little boy.

She felt the prince's eyes on her as she emerged from a cabin wearing the navy maillot she had bought on a recent shopping trip with Laura. It was far more modest than the bikini she'd worn when he fished her out of the sea, but the high cut of the legs and the plunging back were revealing enough, and the lycra fabric skimmed her curves like a second skin.

She fought down a sensation of nearly drowning in Lorne's compelling gaze. He was admiring his property, she told herself fiercely. He had already made it clear that one didn't make love to a bonded servant.

This bond business was the pits, and she wondered how she was going to get through the remainder of her sentence. However loose a rein Lorne kept on her, allowing outings like shopping with Laura and sight-seeing trips with Nori, she couldn't forget her position, as last night had proved. A flash of insight made her frown. Was she really chafing at the restriction on her freedom or because the bond outlawed closeness between her and the prince?

No way, she vowed mentally. The bond had saved her from getting in deeper with Lorne when nothing could come of it. All the same her throat dried and she swallowed hard as he stood up, every muscle gleaming, his black swimming suit molded to hips as hard as angle iron. She was thankful when Nori joined them in the saloon. "Are the dolphins here yet?"

She dragged her gaze to the little boy. "Let's find out."

She wasn't nervous about swimming in the open ocean, having done it off her native Queensland all her life. So why did she tremble when Lorne held out his hand to help her down to the swimming platform?

A crewman fitted them with masks and snorkels. The little boy also wore a flotation vest and listened intently to his father's lecture about the need to hold either his or Allie's hand in the water. "Remember our lessons and turn over on your back to float if you get tired," Lorne told Nori. The child nodded earnestly.

Snorkeling in the aqua waters was heavenly. Zebra and angel fish brushed by in schools, and Allie stared spellbound through the mask at the view of coral and giant clams far below. Then suddenly a pod of spotted dolphins swooped in to surround her and Nori who had taken her hand and floated alongside her.

Her initial lurch of fear gave way to wonder as the gunmetal-gray creatures with their distinctive leopard spots swam and corkscrewed around them. Their faces were set in a perpetual toothy smile she could feel mirrored on her own face.

One of the rare creatures hovered level with Nori's face mask, almost touching the glass with its white-tipped bottle nose. The little boy was beside himself with excitement. It was hard to believe that something weighing over five hundred pounds could be so gentle and playful.

A young dolphin, still to develop spots, came too close to them and was shepherded away by an anxious mother, reminding Allie of herself when she was out with Nori. She smiled at the young prince as he ran a hand across a dolphin's back, his small face alight with wonder behind his mask.

Lorne hovered in the water beside them. She couldn't see his expression but he had to be smiling. With a nod of reassurance to Allie, he took Nori's hand and they swam a little way off, following the pod.

The tableau caught at her. The dolphin family were so involved and protective of each other, their closeness a joy to behold. If only she and the man she loved could be as close.

The man she loved. The thought hit home with such force that she sucked air in through her breathing tube and had to surface to clear it. Gasping and treading water, she faced the truth. In spite of everything, she had done the unthinkable and fallen in love with Lorne. Not the prince, but the man, she recognized painfully, understanding why she had yearned to give herself to him last night and why his rejection was so hard to bear.

On his side it wasn't love as much as physical need born of being alone for too long, she felt sure. As soon as he came to his senses he had retreated behind his great wall of status. Whether she liked it or not, the prince was the larger part of the man she loved, the part forever beyond her reach.

After making sure Nori was safe in his father's care, she lifted herself out of the water onto the swimming platform and stood under a shower to wash off the salt water. No reason a cold shower couldn't work for a woman as well as a man, she thought grimly. In fact it only made her shiver and want him all the more.

By the time Lorne and Nori emerged from the water, she had dried off and changed into white Bermuda shorts and a cerise T-shirt and was sipping a cold drink in the saloon. Oblivious of his wet state Nori raced up the steps and threw himself into Allie's arms, leaving a soggy trail as he climbed onto her lap and linked his baby arms around her neck. "Did you see? Did you see me pat the dolphin? He liked me."

In spite of her inner turmoil or maybe because of it, she wrapped her arms around the small, damp body. Her heart felt as if it was being squeezed in a vise. Her eyes felt bright and she had to blink furiously to bring her emotions back under control. "I saw you, sweetheart," she agreed, her voice husky and vibrant. "One of the dolphins came right up to you to say hello so he must have liked you."

Nori touched a finger to his nose. "He was this close. He had a white nose and lots of sharp teeth but he wasn't scary at all."

She laughed and hugged him tightly. "You're the bravest boy in Carramer and quite possibly also the wettest. Let's get you showered and dried off." Luckily it was so warm that she didn't have to worry about him catching cold.

Lorne was toweling himself dry when they returned to the swimming platform where the shower and dressing rooms were located. She was disturbingly aware of her damp T-shirt clinging to her, outlining every curve. She wished she'd had the presence of mind to protect herself with a towel before Nori had launched himself at her.

Knowing she loved Lorne made it almost impossible to share such a confined space with him without her senses running riot. His amazing body, starkly outlined in the merest scrap of wet lycra, put thoughts in her head that had no business being there. Was her wet T-shirt putting similar thoughts into his head?

His expression gave her no clues as he took in her damp state. "I gather Nori couldn't wait to tell you his news," he said as the little boy splashed in the freshwater shower.

She nodded, not trusting her voice.

"You mean a lot to him," he said.

Safe ground. "He means a lot to me. He's a special little boy." With a special father, insisted a traitorous inner voice. Part of her willed Lorne to return to the saloon while another part longed for him to stay.

"He needs a mother."

It was the last thing she had expected Lorne to say, and her mouth dropped open. An abyss yawned at her feet. Was he going to tell her he had someone in mind? She shot a warning glance in Nori's direction before turning off the shower.

Lorne's look of disgust told her he was well aware that it wasn't a subject to bring up in front of his son. "We'll talk after lunch while Nori has his nap." He ruffled his son's glossy hair.

Nori's small face wrinkled. "Don't want a nap."

"Neither did the baby dolphin, but you saw his mother come and get him, didn't you?" Allie asked.

The little boy nodded. "Was he going to have a nap, too?"

"You bet he was."

The child gave a long-suffering sigh. "I s'pose it's all right then." She was aware of Lorne watching her intently as she shepherded Nori upstairs. Discussing the prince's love life held almost zero appeal now she knew how much she loved him herself. Having slotted her back into the role of servant, he was probably blissfully unaware that it would be a refined form of torture.

What advice could she possibly give? He was right. Nori did need a mother, and she knew just the candidate for the job. But with it came a small detail called marriage to Lorne himself, and that was out of the question.

So was the hope that he would forget the discussion by the time lunch was over. She dawdled over tucking Nori up in one of the spacious cabins, but when she emerged Lorne was waiting on the afterdeck with chilled champagne and glasses set out on a low table between two comfortable chairs. An awning provided shade from the tropical heat, and the sea was like a sheet of glass around the vessel.

She settled into the seat he pulled out for her and accepted a glass of champagne. Dutch courage, she thought ruefully, sipping it. The silence lengthened until her nerves reached screaming point. Her mind insisted on picturing him in the arms of some other woman, triggering a wave of possessiveness that strangled her breathing. Lorne could never belong to her in any sense of the word, but the problem was convincing her emotions.

"You seem on edge," he commented quietly.

She wanted to laugh at the understatement. She was like the proverbial cat on hot bricks. "You had something you wanted to discuss with me, Your Highness?" she asked, desperate to have this over with.

"Titles are hardly appropriate between us, given what I have in mind," he said in a low voice. "I have decided to ask you to marry me."

She almost choked on the champagne. "Marry you? Aren't there laws against it? I'm still bonded to you, after all." She was babbling, she knew, but the blunt proposition had robbed her of coherent speech.

"You suggested the solution yourself last night," he reminded her. "I hereby release you of all obligations under the bond. Think of it as time off for good behavior."

She could barely deal with the restoration of her freedom. Her mind was too busy fixating on his marriage proposal. "Why on earth would you want to marry me?" she asked.

His expression softened. "You are beautiful, skilled in the social graces as my consort must be, and above all, you are good for my son."

"But surely a nanny—"

"He has a nanny," he said, not letting her finish. "What he does not have is a mother."

She found her voice with an effort. "I can't be his mother, as much as I wish I could."

"The instinct for motherhood is not only biological. I see it in the way you behave with him, and he responds to you. You would make an excellent mother for my son."

But what about a wife for Lorne himself? Her thoughts whirled, rejecting his proposal with every fiber of her being. Much as she loved Nori and would give almost anything to be a mother to him, the thought of being Lorne's wife when he didn't love her was intolerable.

"It won't work," she said softly. "It would only be your first marriage all over again."

He shook his head. "Last time I chose with my heart, not my head. This time will be different."

Because he wasn't in love with her, she concluded, wounded beyond belief. Her fingers tightened around the stem of the crystal goblet, and she had to fight the urge to fling the contents over him. Couldn't he see he was asking the impossible?

"It would be an ideal solution for us both," he went on, not giving her chance to argue. "Neither of us wishes to be bound by love. You would have the life you want, free of all responsibility except as my wife and Nori's mother."

Her throat ached. He had reached the wrong conclusion about her, and she had only herself to blame. "You seem very sure I don't want any responsibility."

One dark eyebrow canted upward. "Don't you? Isn't it why you've never tied yourself to a serious relationship before, and why you came to Carramer?"

She wasn't going to marry him, but it was no reason to let him go on believing a lie. "It may look that way to you, but it isn't true. I had years of responsibility long before I should have." Haltingly she explained about her father's desertion and how she had been forced to shoulder his responsibilities at an age when most girls were more concerned with dresses and dates.

He drew a deep breath. "My poor Allie. What was your family thinking to let you take on such burdens?"

"It's in the past now," she said dismissively. "My mother has remarried and is happy at last, and now that my sister has to pay her own way at university, she's finally buckling down to her studies. All's well that ends well."

"Except for you. Who is going to give you back your lost teenage years?" He sounded angry, although she had trouble believing it was on her account.

"Maybe that's why I came to Carramer, to enjoy being young and carefree for a while," she explained, fully understanding her own motives for the first time.

"I see why marriage to me is so hard to contemplate," he volunteered. "You are finally free of all ties, so new ones cannot seem very appealing."

They could but not for the reasons he was offering them. If he had only said he wanted to marry her because he loved her, how different her answer would have been. The memory of her parents constantly arguing, before her father finally moved out, were too vivid for her to consider a loveless marriage. It wouldn't be loveless on her side, but admitting it would only complicate things so she inclined her head in agreement.

"You're right, I do want to be carefree for a while. In any case, you can't order someone to fall in love with you by royal decree."

He sipped champagne thoughtfully before asking, "Why not?"

It was so typically Lorne that she suppressed a smile. What must it be like to have the world turn at your whim? A pang shot through her. It could be her world, too, if she accepted his proposal. From Laura she had learned that there was no such thing as divorce on Carramer, so they would be joined for a lifetime. He could be her husband and lover forever.

Her stomach knotted, and she felt her cheeks catch fire. Thinking of Lorne as her lover for a night was enough to set her nerve endings jangling. Forever was a miracle beyond imagining.

You started this, she told herself, frantically groping for an answer. Nori had already suffered through the loss of his mother and had probably sensed the end of his parents' love long before. Children were like little antennae, picking up emotional vibrations long before they could understand the meaning, Allie knew, both from her teaching experience and her own childhood.

Although years had passed, she vividly recalled the night her father had come to tell her he was leaving. She had known at some level for ages. It hadn't stopped her hoping with all her heart that he wouldn't go. Or that he and her mother would magically fall in love again. They hadn't and Allie had been devastated, driven to pick up the pieces of her world as it fell crazily apart. Part of her was still fighting to hold her world together.

Now she felt the same sense of balancing on a crumbling edge, but she could answer Lorne without betraying too much of her inner turmoil. "It wouldn't be a good example for Nori," she said.

Lorne sat in silence for a long time before asking, "What do you think would set a better example for my son?"

She longed to tell him that Nori needed parents who loved each other and him, who were so obviously in love that it radiated from them, encompassing their child—children, if they were so blessed—and spilled over into the life around them.

Was it so much to hope for? Perhaps she idealized love because of the lack of it in her own family, but she didn't want to change. There had to be something better to aim for than the kind of marriage her parents and Lorne had endured. She couldn't accept that people were meant to settle for second best, when true love existed in the world.

"A wife isn't something you hire, like a nanny or a companion," she told Lorne carefully, her voice clogged with emotion. She coughed to clear it. "Stop thinking of it as filling a vacancy and listen to your heart. To me it sounds as if the prince is doing all the thinking, when a decision like this should be up to the man."

"They are one and the same," he insisted.

She twisted to look at him and regretted it as soon as her gaze collided with his. Her breath came out ragged. She loved him with all her heart. He wanted to marry her. She must be insane to say no. Her emotions churned and she held to her resolve with the last of her courage. Lorne might think the prince and the man were the same, but she knew they weren't.

The prince had been born to his role, trained and groomed to put his people and his duty before everything else. Why else would he propose to Allie if not out of a sense of duty, to provide his son with a mother regardless of his own feelings? She didn't even know what his feelings were, and she wondered if he did.

"That's exactly why I can't marry you," she said, astonished at how hard it was to say the words. Perhaps because it was the opposite of what her heart wanted to say. "I'm not cut out to be royal, sharing my husband with a kingdom. I want..." She couldn't continue. What she really wanted and what he was willing to provide were worlds apart.

"You want to be courted," he said, misunderstanding. "Of course, I should have seen it before."

She gave him a slightly dazed look, her pulse thundering in her ears. "What are you talking about?"

He turned his body until his knees almost touched hers. "Tell me how your ideal romance would unfold in your country."

Her mind whirled. She had drunk only a little champagne, but the buzz in her head suggested it was having an effect. Or else it was his nearness making her body feel like a tuning fork, vibrating with unspoken needs. Her mind struggled to block the sensations, but they flooded through her uncontrollably until she leaned toward him as if drawn by an invisible thread.

She ran her tongue over dry lips. "Yes, my ideal romance includes being courted," she heard herself admit as if from a long way away. "My love would bring me flowers and champagne. We'd talk softly over candlelit dinners for two. And gradually we'd learn how important we are to each other and how little meaning life would have if we were forced to be apart."

"Would you kiss?"

A lump rose in her throat. "It's what people do when they're in love." He had kissed her and he wasn't in love with her, she thought, contradicting herself. But this wasn't real, this was her fantasy, and kissing was definitely called for.

Her voice vibrated and her eyes were moist by the time she'd finished painting the word picture. She must be crazy sharing her fantasy with him when nothing of the sort was going to happen. He was right. The prince and the man were one. The man might contemplate a slow, intimate dance of courtship such as she had described, but the prince was too bound by protocol.

Was that what had gone wrong in his first marriage? Had he been too inflexible, commanding a result rather than working to create understanding between him and his wife? Allie could hardly blame him if so. From boyhood he had been raised knowing he would become the sovereign of his country. Asking nicely for what he wanted was probably as alien to him as issuing orders would be to her.

"You seem very sure of what you want," Lorne observed tautly. He didn't sound pleased, and she wondered if he would have preferred her to specify diamonds and rubies as the price of her love. At least then he would have known what to do.

"I am sure," she confirmed, wishing with all her heart that she didn't mean it. But there was no escaping it. Being who and what he was, he couldn't give her what she needed, and she couldn't give him what he wanted.

Impasse.

He took the champagne glass from her, his fingers brushing hers in a butterfly touch, and her stomach muscles clenched. Forestalling tears became a full-time job for the next few minutes. Loving him and knowing it couldn't lead anywhere was almost more than she could stand.

Somehow she had to stand it, at least until she could put some distance between them. As long as he was only a heartbeat away and she could feel his breath fanning her cheek, she hadn't a prayer of refusing him for long.

In that same moment it came to her that she was free. In order to propose, Lorne had released her from the bond. A stab of anguish caught her unawares. Surely she didn't want to remain tied to him, knowing there was no future in it? As a free woman she could take up the reins of her life again, move on, find someone who could truly love her.

It wasn't as much consolation as she thought it should be.

Chapter Eleven

The first thing that hit Allie when she opened the door to her suite was the scent of orchids, lots and lots of orchids.

She pushed the door wider and stopped in openmouthed amazement. Every surface in the sitting room was covered with vases of the delicate, wonderfully fragrant native orchids that Carramer was famous for. It looked as if an entire season's crop was right here in her room.

Long stems, small sprays, single blooms—they brimmed from silver and gold bowls and vases of antique porcelain, Lladro glass and Baccarat crystal. Dazedly she did a circuit of the room, touching one or two vessels to assure herself she wasn't dreaming.

It was the same in the bedroom. The heavy antique furniture was almost hidden by bouquets of the tiny orchids known as ladies' slippers, after their dainty shape. As a final touch, rose petals were scattered across the bed.

"Lorne," she said aloud. She might have known he wouldn't give up so easily. While they sailed back to Turtle Bay aboard the ketch, he must have had the captain send word to the summer palace to have the flowers waiting in her suite when they got home.

The extravagance of the gesture was breathtaking. Even given Lorne's vast royal powers it was no small achievement to round up so many flowers in the few hours it had taken them to sail back to Turtle Bay and return by helicopter to the main island.

"Somewhere on Celeste there's an orchid farm without a single flower to its name," she muttered, disturbing rose petals as she sank onto the bed. Their fragrance rose in a cloud around her, unbelievably seductive. Her response gave a new meaning to the term hot and bothered. She felt hot because she had never been so flagrantly courted in her life, and bothered because it was for all the wrong reasons.

"Lorne de Marigny, why can't you take no for an answer?" she asked the scented air. What was next? She wracked her brains to recall the requirements she had outlined for ideal courtship when they discussed it on the ketch. Apart from flowers, the only other things she could think of were intimate conversation over a candlelit dinner and—had she mentioned champagne?

"No, he wouldn't." On a surge of foreboding, she burst into the marble bathroom opening off her bedroom. Fewer flowers adorned the bathroom, but the enormous whirlpool bath was filled to the brim and bubbling merrily. She dipped a finger into the tub and touched it to her mouth. "Champagne," she groaned. The sheer extravagance of it reminded her starkly of whom she was dealing with.

For a giddy moment she considered undressing and climbing into the whirlpool just so she could say she had bathed in champagne. Then the seriousness of the situation overtook her. Lorne wasn't just courting her, he was trying to overwhelm her defenses, and she was very much afraid he would succeed if she didn't put a stop to it right now.

Without giving herself time to change out of her sailing

clothes or reconsider the wisdom of confronting the country's ruler, she flung herself out of the flower-decked suite and went in search of the prince.

She found him enjoying a glass of sherry on the terrace with Dr. Pascale. The prince looked pleased when she appeared, taking in her shorts and T-shirt with every sign of appreciation. "I'll ring for another glass."

"No, thanks," she snapped, earning a curious look from the doctor. She would have preferred not to have an audience, but if she retreated now she might never have the nerve to confront Lorne again. "What do you think you're doing, Your Highness?" she demanded through clenched teeth.

His expression softened. "I take it you've found the flowers and the champagne."

"Found them? I couldn't miss them if I tried. I think my possessions are in there somewhere, but all I could see when I walked in were flowers. As for the champagne, haven't you heard that there are starving people in the world? For the cost of the stuff filling my tub, you could probably feed dozens of them for a week."

"It isn't vintage," he said, sounding slightly shaken.

She refused to be sidetracked. "That's not the point. It's too much. Way too much."

Alain Pascale coughed quietly. "Told you so."

They both whirled on him and said in unison. "Please keep out of this, Doctor."

Unperturbed, the older man held up his hands. "Gladly." He picked up his sherry glass and edged around them, a wry grin tugging at the corners of his mouth. "If you two lovebirds will excuse me, I'll finish this in the library."

The glass door whispered shut behind the doctor and Allie glared at Lorne. Whatever his feelings might be toward her, *lovebirds* wasn't the word she would use to describe them. He had the grace to look discomfited but she might have known that backing down wasn't in the royal repertoire. "On the yacht when I asked how you wanted to be courted, you said with flowers and champagne," he reminded her.

Her jaw clenched. "We were discussing a hypothetical courtship."

"Then—hypothetically—how many flowers would be enough? How much champagne would be just right before you could accept my proposal of marriage?"

She sighed with frustration. "Marriage isn't something you do by numbers, or at least I don't. I'm touched by the trouble you went to over the flowers, honestly. And the champagne in the spa. I was seriously tempted to try a dip."

His eyes gleamed as if he was imagining her with champagne bubbles lapping her breasts. "What stopped you?"

He had, for a start. "I don't want lavish gifts from you. They only have meaning when they come with—" about to say *with love*, she bit the words back in time "—with some feeling behind them, preferably mutual. Otherwise they're empty gestures. Grand gestures, but still empty."

He looked thoughtful. "Mutual and with feeling? How can you tell?"

The trap yawned but she was too worked up to see it. "When you touch, you feel something for each other."

He moved closer. Before she had time to prepare, he closed the remaining distance between them and gathered her into his arms. "You mean like this?"

She tried to hold herself stiffly but it was no use. The pressure of his hands against the small of her back collapsed her lungs in a rush. As she opened her mouth to pull in air he took advantage of the moment to kiss her fiercely. Heat tore through her like wildfire. She couldn't help herself. Into her answering kiss she poured all the love she didn't feel safe enough to put into words.

Fool, she told herself in the distant corner of her mind where sanity still prevailed. She had intended to fling his gifts back at him, tell him they weren't her price. She hadn't counted on him knowing exactly what her price was and paying it in coin she hadn't the strength to refuse.

The sense of lost control was terrifying. How could she feel this way with a man who wanted her but not her love? She was too aware of the damage a loveless marriage could inflict, not only on the two people concerned but on their children. She remembered vividly how empty and helpless she had felt. As an adult she would never willingly put herself through it again.

Her body had other ideas. As her knees threatened to buckle, she clung to him, feeling his muscles surge under her fingers. Other parts were surging, too, and she shivered as she became aware of her effect on him. He wasn't the only one. She felt almost unbearably aroused. Like a sleep-walker she parted the white silk of his shirt and plunged her hands beneath it, running them over his washboard stomach and up to where his heart throbbed in erratic counterpoint to her own.

His breathing became labored and his fingers threaded through her hair, urging her head back until she was literally panting in front of him. His mouth fastened on hers in a quick, fierce kiss that felt shockingly possessive. Before she had fully absorbed it, he lifted his head. "Now tell me you don't feel anything for me."

Like a splash of cold water, his words jolted her back to reality. What was she doing? For a few heart-stopping moments Lorne had made her forget why this could never work. Now it was time to come down to earth. "What I feel has nothing to do with it," she said, aware of how prim she sounded, like the schoolmarm she actually was. It was a timely thought, since her teaching background was part of the reason Lorne regarded her as a suitable mother for his son. Finding her physically attractive was probably a bonus.

It was one of the hardest steps she had ever taken, but she backed away, forcing him to untangle his fingers from her hair. For long moments the strands formed a silken link between them. He let her hair flow like a river through his fingers, seeming loath to let it go. She expelled an uneven breath. "Did you mean it when you said I was released from my bond?"

His chest lifted, and he sighed deeply. "Under our law I couldn't ask you to marry me while you were still bonded to me."

Her heart constricted. "Then my freedom is conditional?"

His eyes were bleak. "No, although I wish it could be."

She didn't have to ask why. No doubt having her indentured to him was more convenient than freeing her to make choices he considered wrong. He would probably have liked to order her to marry him, but for once Carramer law was on her side. It didn't feel much like a victory.

What she really wanted was to throw herself into his arms and hear him say he loved her. Since it wasn't going to happen, there was only one course open to her. "Now that I'm free, I've decided to go to Solano to continue my vacation," she said before her courage deserted her. "Will you accept my resignation, effective immediately, Your Highness?"

"Do I have a choice?" he said, so bitterly that she looked at him in shock. Was she wrong about why he wanted her to stay? He soon disabused her. "Nori is going to miss you."

But not Lorne himself, she noted despondently. "He still has Laura Myss for company. In any case, she tells me you'll be returning to the capital yourself soon," she said as brightly as she could. "I'm looking forward to seeing the city."

"Do you have somewhere to stay?" he asked huskily.

She nodded, hoping he wouldn't invite her to stay at the palace. It was hard enough walking away once without putting herself through the ordeal again. "Laura has offered me the use of her family's apartment. She introduced me to the owner of a gallery in Solano, and he has accepted some of my paintings for exhibition. I don't expect them to sell as I'm an unknown, but it will be exciting to see my work on show."

"No regrets, no second thoughts?" he asked.

If he only knew. "I've enjoyed working for you and Nori, Your Highness," she said, deliberately misunderstanding.

His brow furrowed. "Damn it, Allie, I don't make a habit of proposing to my staff. You know you're more than an employee to me."

Thinking of the Heaven she had so nearly found in his arms, she knew the feeling was very, very mutual. She still felt tied to him, not by law, but by the force of her love for him. She waited tensely, hoping against hope for some sign that he felt the same. When he remained silent, she knew it was over.

She turned away to hide her brimming eyes. "I'll talk to Nori tomorrow and make sure he understands why I have to go."

Lorne muttered something that sounded suspiciously like, "If he does, that will make one of us," but she fled before she gave in to the temptation to ask him to elaborate.

After the tranquillity of Allora and the royal villa, Allie found Solano crowed, colorful and bustling, but its subtropical atmosphere so reminded her of her native Brisbane that she felt instantly at home.

Located on a peninsula in the northwestern region of Celeste, the city was strung, jewel-like, along a series of bays, giving it a charmingly open feel and glorious ocean views from almost every part. So Allie wasn't surprised that Laura's family's apartment enjoyed a sea view even though it was located in the city's commercial area, near a central square lined with coconut and flame trees.

The only drawback was the presence of the royal palace on a promontory overlooking the square. It was obviously designed to be prominent with its distinctive marriage of European and Pacific architecture, the curved roof supposedly representing an upturned canoe. But it meant that every time Allie returned to Laura's apartment she felt as if Lorne himself was looking over her shoulder.

The blue-and-jade Carramer flag flying above the palace meant the prince was back in residence, the building concierge told her excitedly, as he held the door for her. She could have gone her whole life without knowing that, she thought unhappily. Somehow it was easier to think of Lorne and Nori at the villa, than so close by she might run into them at any time.

She wasn't going to run into the prince in the street, she told herself firmly. He was the country's ruler, sheltered from everyday life by his position and a phalanx of minders. Even if she took the tour of the palace that she had read about in a guide book, she wouldn't necessarily see Lorne. His offices and private apartments would be located well away from the rooms the public were allowed to see.

She pushed the thought from her mind. She was not—repeat not—going anywhere near the palace. It was almost six and she had an appointment with the owner of the gallery where her paintings were being shown.

The prospect gave her spirits a lift. Anton, the owner, was not only enthusiastic about her work, he had agreed to show almost everything she had painted while she was at the villa. His highest praise had been reserved for the portrait of Lorne. She hadn't wanted it shown, fearing that it revealed too much of her state of mind. But Anton had insisted, refusing to hang anything else until she gave in.

So here she was, three weeks after leaving Lorne's employ, steeling herself to face him on canvas, as the centerpiece of her work. Anton beamed as he met her at the gallery entrance. He kissed her on both cheeks in the Carramer way and grasped her hands tightly, steering her toward the room where her paintings were displayed.

"I have a surprise for you, my dear," he said indulgently. He was a close friend of Laura Myss's family and a surrogate uncle to Laura, and had appointed himself to a similar role for Allie. It hadn't influenced his judgment of her work, he had assured her, but it meant they could be friends as well as business associates. She was touched, feeling as if she needed friends right now.

"What's going on?" she asked, hearing the excitement in Anton's tone. "Don't tell me someone has bought one of my paintings."

"Better than that," he bubbled. "See for yourself."

At the door of the small room containing her paintings, he stopped and pushed Allie a little ahead of himself. At first she noticed nothing amiss except the uncomfortable feeling that Lorne was watching her from the portrait. It was uncannily lifelike, even she had to admit. Painting someone with love had its advantages.

Then she saw what Anton was so excited about, and her jaw dropped. "They can't *all* be sold," she said in amazement, noting the small stickers adhering to every frame. "Who would buy so many works by an unknown artist from Australia?"

Anton didn't have to tell her. Somehow she knew. She shook her head in violent negation. "No, I've decided they're not for sale, after all.'' Especially not to Lorne de Marigny.

Anton looked shocked. "You can't withdraw them now. My buyer—"

"Is Prince Lorne, I know," she said, gaining confirmation from the sudden flush on Anton's features. "He doesn't really want to buy my paintings. He wants to buy me."

"Correct on all counts," drawled an all-too-familiar voice.

Her knees went weak. Anton immediately bowed deeply. "Your Highness, this is an unexpected pleasure. I wasn't informed you intended to visit."

"I hadn't decided myself until you informed me that the artist would be calling on you today," Lorne said easily, his gaze locking with Allie's. "I'm delighted I did. It's good to see you again, Allie. Nori has missed you."

But not Lorne himself, she noticed with a pang. Anton looked impressed. From Laura he knew that Allie had been employed by the royal family, but that was all. That *was* all, Allie reminded herself. It didn't stop her soaking up every detail of Lorne's appearance like someone offered food after a long fast. He looked impossibly healthy, tanned and strong. Yet she read new lines of strain around his eyes and mouth. Imagination, she told herself, hoping he couldn't see the same "imaginary" strain in her.

"How is Nori, Your Highness?" she asked, keeping her tone carefully neutral.

His eyes darkened, but he bowed fractionally. "He is well, although he asks after you every day. I hope starting school will take his mind off your absence."

She felt her own eyes widen. "You're allowing him to go to school?"

His gaze impaled her. "A good ruler knows when to take expert advice."

Her advice? She could hardly believe she had had such an effect on him. It wasn't in her to gloat, not when her greater failure outweighed her small success. The proof was right here in front of her, hurting her to the depths of her being. "I'm glad for Nori's sake," she said softly. "Please give him my love?"

"I would rather give him much more."

She passed a hand across her eyes. "Please, Lor...Your Highness, we've been over this. Buying my paintings won't change anything."

Lorne's face was stone. "Then you should have no problem having dinner with me this evening. To finalize the details of my purchase," he added, possibly for Anton's sake.

She had forgotten the gallery owner, hovering solicitously at her side. Lorne had gambled that she wouldn't argue with him in front of Anton. As usual the prince was right. "Very well, I'll have dinner with you—to discuss the paintings," she conceded, wondering what she was getting herself into.

For the first time she noticed that Lorne had arrived alone. No minders hovered at his elbow or ranged around the gallery, their eyes taking in everyone and everything around them. Lorne himself looked subtly different, she became aware. He was impeccably dressed in a charcoal business suit and snow-white shirt with a burgundy tie, but there were no monograms in evidence, nothing suggesting regal status. He might have been an ordinary man asking her out on an ordinary date.

Except they both knew he wasn't.

It was a strange experience being escorted to a restaurant on the arm of a prince without anyone recognizing who he was. Lorne had chosen, deliberately, she suspected, an out-of-the-way French bistro where the lights were so low they had to grope their way to a table.

"You booked the table under my name," she commented, uncomfortably thinking that he had been very sure of her acceptance.

In the gloom she couldn't be sure, but it looked as if he smiled. "I could hardly reserve it under mine."

"I suppose not." She leaned across to him although few of the neighboring tables were occupied at this early hour. In Carramer it was more usual to dine late. "Do you do this sort of thing often?"

"You are the first woman I have gone out with privately since my days at university," he told her.

"I mean sneak out of the palace and move around incognito," she amended, refusing to let herself feel flattered at being singled out for his attention. If he hadn't, she wouldn't have to deal with nerves that jangled like alarm bells and a lurching sensation in the pit of her stomach that would make eating anything a challenge.

"You've seen too many romantic movies," he said dryly. "The security risks in such behavior are enormous. In any case, I can learn as much about my people's moods and desires from reading the popular press as from wandering the streets."

Yet he had taken the risk to meet her. "Why are you doing this?" she asked, unable to bear the suspense a moment longer.

"I wanted to see you," he said simply.

"But why? Nothing has changed between us. You're still the ruler of Carramer, and I'm still a commoner from Australia." And there was still no love between them, she added inwardly.

"Not tonight," he pointed out. "Tonight I am an ordinary businessman, dining with a beautiful woman." He glanced around at the few occupied tables. "No one is paying us the slightest attention. Can't you simply enjoy the experience for one night?''

It gave a whole new meaning to the term *one-night stand,* she thought as a tremor shook her. He had turned the Cinderella tradition on its head, becoming a commoner dining with Cinders, except that he would turn back into a prince at midnight and she would still be Cinders. All the same he was offering her a wonderful fantasy, and she was as tempted to accept as she had ever been.

She knew she should get up from the chair and walk away as far as her legs would carry her. It wasn't all that far, she soon found. Her leg muscles locked her in place, denying her mental command to rise. The moment his fingers curled around hers across the table, she was lost. It was exactly the way she had dreamed of being with him, so why shouldn't she make the most of it? After today it was all she would ever have to remember him by. ''Very well,'' she agreed. ''But only for one evening.''

It was an evening out of a fairy tale. Lorne might not choose to be a prince tonight, but to Allie his status informed every move he made. How could the other patrons not recognize his air of authority and personal power? ''You even order food royally,'' she commented.

''You mean I lack grace or humility?'' He sounded concerned.

''Not at all. But ordinary people don't have your confidence and assurance,'' she said. ''Even when you're trying not to, you sound like you rule. I guess you have to be born to it.''

''Is that why you won't marry me?''

So far she had managed to keep the conversation on neutral ground, discussing Nori, her paintings and her stay in Solano. She might have known it couldn't last. Like the air before a thunderstorm, the atmosphere felt charged. The storm had to break sometime.

"I can't marry you because you don't love me," she admitted. "Call me sentimental, but I don't want a marriage of convenience."

His hand found hers again on the tablecloth, and his index finger traced a circle in her palm. Shivers raced along her spine. "It would hardly be a marriage of convenience. You already know how much I want you, Allie."

She did know and, pity help her, she wanted him. The mere thought of sharing his bed set flames of desire leaping through her. She fought them. He still hadn't said the three words she needed to hear. "Marriage isn't only about sex," she insisted. "It's also about two people wanting so much to share their lives that they'll do anything, give up anything, in order to be together."

"Can't I feel that way about you?"

She shook her head. "I think you'd like to, but your position keeps getting in the way." She glanced around, feeling choked. "This is a moment out of time, it can't last. I shouldn't have agreed to come with you."

His fingers locked around her wrist before she could pull away. "You did agree. Why, Allie?"

She choked off a sob. "Because I..." I love you. For a horrific moment she thought she'd said it aloud, but thankfully it was only in her head. "I was curious," she said instead.

"Now you've satisfied your curiosity, it's over." His voice sounded clipped, royal again. He had turned back into the prince, she realized with a sinking heart. She had achieved her goal of convincing him she didn't care, and she wanted to die.

He stood up and dropped some large bills onto the table, not bothering to wait for change. "I'll take you home."

Chapter Twelve

He was as good as his word, keeping a discreet distance as he walked beside her along the darkened streets toward the building housing Laura's family apartment. It must have been as rare for him to walk the streets at night as it was for her, but he didn't show it.

She was the one having problems. She saw potential assassins around every corner, tensing automatically whenever a stranger came up behind them. Finally Lorne asked her why she was so jumpy.

Telling him the truth would reveal how much she cared about him. "It's my Aussie upbringing," she said instead. "Brisbane isn't exactly the crime capital of the world, but women have to watch where they go at night."

"It wouldn't be because I told you I'm taking a security risk by coming out unguarded?"

She forced a laugh and shook her head. "I'm sure you can take care of yourself. You're a big boy." She felt weak, thinking of how true it was.

"Self-defense was part of my education," he agreed. "I'm glad you're not concerned on my account."

He didn't sound glad, she noted. He sounded as if he had retreated behind his great wall of status again. She was achingly aware that the prince walked beside her, not Lorne, the man she loved. What did she expect? He was what he was, and she wouldn't change him if she could. Her own feelings were another matter.

He insisted on riding with her up to her floor and waiting while she opened the front door. On the threshold she hesitated, unable to put into words the sense of loss crashing through her. This might be the last time she ever saw him. "Lorne, I—"

"Yes?"

"Thank you for a pleasant evening." How stupidly formal she sounded, when everything in her wanted to invite him in and make sure he didn't want to leave for the longest time.

His dark gaze slid down the length of her body as if he was committing her to memory. "My pleasure, Allie. Have a safe journey home." He dropped his hands to her shoulders, bent his head and pressed a kiss to her forehead, the touch of his mouth burning like a brand.

Then he was gone, and she was alone on the doorstep, staring at the empty spot where he had stood and wishing for a miracle. They never arrived when you needed them, she recalled, thinking of her unhappy childhood. She had wished for a miracle to reunite her mother and father, but it hadn't happened. The one she coveted now—for Lorne to love her—was even less likely. Fighting back tears, she went inside.

She awoke from a restless night with one thought in her head, to get as far away from Carramer and Lorne as she could. Making herself coffee, she sat down beside the telephone and called the airline, managing to secure a seat on an afternoon flight back to Australia.

Her next call was to Anton at the gallery, to give him the details of the Brisbane bank where he could forward the proceeds of her paintings. He sounded relieved that she wasn't going to argue about the sale, but it no longer mattered. Lorne had already seen his portrait, painted with all the love in her soul. If he was so blind to the message in it, she didn't care if she never set eyes on it again.

Should she call Lorne at the palace and tell him she was leaving? She decided against it. They had said their good-byes last night. He had even wished her a safe journey home. Home. The term seemed incongruous. As Helen Pascale had said, home was wherever the man she loved happened to be. For Allie, it wasn't Brisbane and never would be again. But she couldn't stay in Carramer, and the city where she was born was as good a destination as anywhere.

She would have to call the palace after all, she realized. She needed to make arrangements to return the apartment keys to Laura Myss. She reached for the phone again and jumped when it rang as her fingers brushed it.

Suppressing a feeling of foreboding, she lifted the receiver. "Hello?"

"Allie, it's Alain Pascale."

Hearing the palace doctor's name, she felt her heart lurch. "Has something happened to Lorne? He isn't ill or anything?"

"He's not ill unless you count taking leave of his senses," the doctor supplied.

"I don't understand. What has he done?"

"It's not what he's done so much as what he's planning to do. He's talking about abdicating his throne in favor of his brother, Michel."

A fist closed suffocatingly around Allie's throat, and darkness fringed her vision. "Abdicate? Why on earth would he do such thing?"

"You tell me," the doctor demanded. "He rang me at

some ungodly hour last night and insisted we share a night-cap, then he told me what was on his mind."

"Why do you think I should know anything about it?" she asked on a sudden suspicion.

"Weren't you with him last night?"

"We had dinner but…oh, mercy!" It came back to her in a rush. She had told him that two people who loved each other would do anything, give up anything, in order to be together. "I didn't mean for him to take me literally," she gasped, almost afraid to wonder what it meant if he had.

"Did you set giving up his throne as the price for marrying you?" the doctor demanded. He sounded furious, his normally kind bedside manner overpowered by worry for his prince.

She was frantic with fear, too. She wanted Lorne's love, but not at the cost of everything he held dear. Sooner or later he would hate her for putting him in such a position. It was better to walk away now than wait until that day came. "I would never dream of setting such a condition," she told the doctor. He probably didn't believe her, but it was the truth.

There was a thoughtful pause. "He evidently thinks you did."

"What can I do?"

"Come and see him, make it clear that you don't want him to abdicate on your account."

She twisted the telephone cord in nerveless fingers. Seeing Lorne again wasn't part of her plans. The very thought tore at her. But she couldn't let him take such a drastic step if there was some way to prevent it. "I'll do what I can," she said heavily.

The doctor's sigh of relief rushed through the line. "Lorne's schedule is clear from eleven until noon. If I send a car for you, can you be here then?"

Even the prince's crises had to be scheduled, she noted

ironically. For a wild moment she was sorely tempted to say no and let Lorne carry out his wish. He would be free to follow his heart. No more schedules. No more demands. He could love her the way she wanted to be loved.

How long would it last if she let him sacrifice his kingdom for her love? She knew the answer in her own heart. Sooner or later the burden of conscience would erode his love for her, and they would be left with nothing. Less than nothing. At least this way she had her own love for him as solace through the long days ahead. "I'll be ready," she told the doctor heavily.

By the time the limousine bearing the royal coat of arms pulled up outside the apartment block, she knew what she had to do. The curious glances of the concierge and the passersby as she was handed into the car went almost unnoticed. She was too preoccupied with a plan that demanded acting ability she wasn't at all sure she possessed.

Could she carry it off? Could she make Lorne think she cared so little for him that abandoning his throne would be a futile gesture? Somehow she had to, or else they were both lost.

Her hands twisted in her lap as the car negotiated the twisting turns to the peak where the palace was located. In the back of the limousine, within arm's reach, a bar offered an assortment of wine, spirits and mixers. Never had she been so sorely tempted to resort to Dutch courage, but she resisted it. What she contemplated was hard enough with a clear head.

Dr. Pascale must have made arrangements because Lorne's aide was expecting her and took her straight in to see the prince. He had aged since last night, she saw with a shock of recognition. She hadn't looked in a mirror for a while. Maybe the strain of last night and this morning was visible on her face, too.

"You look wonderful this morning, Allie," Lorne said.

He came around the desk and took both her hands in his. "I'm glad you're here. I have something to tell you."

Say it now or you never will, she ordered herself. "Me first," she insisted, knowing she sounded overbright, but unable to do anything about it.

He led her to a leather-covered chesterfield and sat her down beside him. "Would you like me to ring for coffee?"

"No, thank you. I haven't much time." His eyebrows lifted curiously and she rushed on, "My flight back to Australia leaves at four."

His expression softened but it was the only part of him that did, she saw from the rigid way he held himself, as if it cost him a lot not to take her in his arms. The feeling was painfully mutual. "If you came to say goodbye, there's no need," he volunteered.

She looked down at her hands, still captive in his, and deliberately pulled them free. "I'm afraid there is. Last night was a mistake. I said some things I didn't mean. I wanted to apologize and set the record straight before I go."

The tension in the room could be cut with a knife. Lorne's eyes never left her face, and the way his features hardened made her want to weep. "You said you wanted to be loved," he reminded her. "I want to love you, not as a prince, but as an ordinary man. I want to give up everything and marry you, Allie."

"As a mother for Nori?" she couldn't resist asking a little bitterly.

"Above all as my wife and the custodian of my heart," he supplied. "Are you telling me you didn't mean it when you said you wanted it, too?"

She affected a light laugh. "I only said it because I knew it was impossible. I can't marry you, because I don't love you, Lorne. Giving up your throne won't change my feelings."

His hard gaze bored into her. "I don't believe you."

He had to believe her, she thought frantically. She had wanted him to love her, but not to give up everything he held dear in the process. She couldn't let him do it, and the only way she could think to stop him was to convince him she didn't care. "You don't want to believe me," she said flatly. "You're so used to commanding everyone that you can't handle being turned down. Can't you see, Lorne, with that attitude you wouldn't last five minutes out in the real world, where nobody is forced to do your bidding."

"Is that what you think?" he asked, bitterness edging his tone. He stood up and paced to the windows where he stood with his back to her, his hands linked behind him as he stared out. "You think I only want you because you're unobtainable? It isn't true." He whirled around. "I want you because you're the only woman I have ever truly loved. Even when my marriage was relatively happy, it never felt like this."

He stalked to the couch and bent close to her, imprisoning her with an arm on each side. His face was very close to hers, and she held her breath. "Alain put you up to this, didn't he?"

She shook her head. "He told me what you planned, but coming here was my own idea."

He cursed softly, as if he had been hoping the blame belonged with Alain. She couldn't let him think so. Even without the doctor's urging, she would have felt bound to try to talk Lorne out of giving up everything for her. It was the right thing, the only thing to do. She only wished it didn't feel so much like the end of the world.

She wished he would move away and give her some badly needed emotional space. With his mouth so close to hers, the memory of his kisses threatened to distract her from what she needed to do. "Must you loom over me? It bothers me," she said.

His mouth twisted into a sardonic smile. "Does it now? If you really don't care about me, it shouldn't bother you at all. Any more than this should."

His kiss was filled with such passion and tenderness that tears flooded her eyes. He saw them and touched a finger to her beaded lashes. "These can't be for me. You don't love me, remember?"

It was becoming harder and harder to remember as he feathered her face and neck with kisses tender enough to melt the hardest heart. Hers wasn't that hard to begin with, and it wasn't the only part she could feel starting to melt. Inside she felt like a glacier at the coming of spring, imagining hundreds of cracks appearing in her resolve and chunks breaking off to join the torrent of sensations pouring through her.

"Lorne, please stop," she implored. "I can't let you do this."

"I'll stop when I get the truth out of you," he said, his voice muffled against her neck.

She tilted her head back and closed her eyes but it was a mistake, only serving to focus her churning senses on how wonderful his touch made her feel. Much more of this and she would break down altogether. With a supreme effort she rallied the last of her defenses. "I'm telling you the truth. Whether you're a prince or a pauper makes no difference. My answer is still the same."

"Then you don't care if I give up the throne?"

"Do what you want."

It was meant to come out offhand but the agony in her voice was a dead giveaway. To her amazement he didn't seem to hear it, but straightened and offered her a hand up. "I guess there's nothing more to be said except goodbye."

She kept her eyes averted so he wouldn't see the moisture blurring them. At the door she said over her shoulder,

"Thanks for the holiday romance, Your Highness. Back home they'll never believe whom I was dating."

Careful, don't overdo it, she cautioned herself, reaching for the heavy brass door handle. It bore the de Marigny coat of arms, she noticed, with the heightened awareness she seemed to have developed around Lorne.

His voice stopped her in her tracks. "Not so fast, Allie. This isn't over yet."

She squared her shoulders. "You've just admitted there's nothing more to be said except goodbye. So…goodbye." Her voice almost broke on the last word but she managed it somehow.

"Turn around."

His voice was laced with royal command backed by centuries of tradition she sensed it would be dangerous to disobey, even for a foreigner. Her limbs felt creaky and stiff as she forced herself to turn.

It was almost her undoing as she faced the evidence of what she had done to him. His face looked flushed, ravaged almost, and his richly tanned skin was filmed with perspiration. He held himself rigidly, his hands clenched into fists at his sides as if he wanted to lash out but couldn't decide at whom. But it was the anguish she read in his eyes that sliced all the way to her soul.

She couldn't hold the words back. "Lorne, don't…"

"I could ask the same of you," he said, his voice so raw with pain that she took a step toward him without conscious awareness only to freeze as he added, "You almost had me fooled until you made that 'holiday romance' crack. This was no more a holiday romance for you than it was for me."

Hope rose in her like a living thing until she crushed it by force of will. "Whatever it was, it's over, Lorne. It has to be. I can't let you give up your throne for me, no matter what I feel."

A glimmer flamed in his eyes. "Then you admit you feel something?"

"Of course I feel something. What do you take me for, a robot?" she threw at him through rapidly blurring vision.

His hands clenched against his thighs as if he controlled himself with an effort. "A robot wouldn't set me on fire the way you do. Nor would she drive me to do insane things."

"Like give up your throne?" It came out as a tortured whisper. He knew, she thought. He knew how she felt, and he wasn't about to let her walk out. Mixed with the elation the thought provoked was despair that she had failed in her mission.

"Like fall in love, something I vowed after my marriage I would never do again as long as I lived."

Her heart bucked so violently she pressed a hand to her chest in alarm. "What are you saying?"

"What do you think? I love you, Allie. If it costs me my crown, my country and everything I own, I'll pursue you until you agree to marry me."

"You won't have to pursue me very far," she said in a tiny voice. She could hardly believe he was finally saying the words she had longed to hear. "I love you, too, with all my heart."

"Allie." He crossed the room in two strides and hauled her against his chest, covering her face with butterfly kisses designed to leave her in no doubt as to how much she was loved. She was gripped by a pleasure so intense it was a hairbreadth away from pain.

Still, she had to know. "How can you love me when I'm everything you dislike in a woman?"

He nodded as if in agreement. "Independent, stubborn, willful and wayward," he ticked off on his fingers under her nose. "Actually, they're qualities I quite like in a woman, as long as she loves me."

The masculine scent of him surrounded her, promising security and dependability, and other delights she didn't dare think about right now. "I do love you," she vowed. "Pretending I didn't was the hardest thing I've ever done."

He feathered kisses over her half-closed eyes, and she sucked in a shuddering breath. "Luckily for me, you're a poor actor."

Her eyes fluttered open. "But you weren't acting, were you? You would really have given up your throne to pursue me." Her voice was filled with the wonder of being so loved and the terror that he would actually have carried out his threat.

He nodded. "I would do whatever it takes to keep you at my side."

"All you have to do is ask me," she urged huskily.

For a moment he hesitated, and she was gripped by panic. What if he didn't intend to ask her again? Panic turned to joy as he dropped to one knee in front of her, one of her hands clasped between both of his. "Alison Carter, will you marry me and rule Carramer at my side, as my princess?"

The enormity of what he was asking threatened to overwhelm her until she looked into his eyes, nearly drowning in the love she saw mirrored there. How could she feel fear when he would be beside her, tutoring her in how to be his princess? Tutoring her in many other arts, as well, she thought, feeling her face catch fire. "Yes to everything, Lorne. All I want is for us to be together."

He released a strangled breath, as if he hadn't been entirely sure of her answer. Then his arms tightened around her. "My Allie, my *amouvere*. From now on my heart and my kingdom are yours to command. Whatever you want you have only to ask."

Suddenly shy, she ducked her head and plucked at his shirtfront with uncertain fingers. It was time to put into practise some of the words Laura had taught her. "All I want is your love, *ma amouvere, ta'ama ta'vera.*"

He chuckled, sliding a finger under her chin and tilting her face up to his. "I adore that you're learning Carramer, but what you said—it isn't 'I love you.' You just invited me to spend a week in your bed."

She felt heat traveling up her neck and into her face but made herself meet his eyes. "So? Do you have a problem with that?"

"Not a one, my princess," he said without missing a beat. "There's nowhere in the world I'd rather be. But since I believe in setting a good example for my people, I'll try to restrain myself until our wedding day. It won't be easy if you insist on issuing invitations like that one."

"I'll try to behave myself, at least until the ceremony," she promised, knowing it wouldn't be easy for her, either.

He became sober suddenly. "You know there's no divorce in our country, so I hope you're very sure it's what you want."

She didn't hesitate. "You are what I want. I sensed it from that moment when the rip you call the serpent washed me up at your feet, but after seeing what hell my parents went through without love, I thought marriage wasn't for me."

"So you pretended not to want the responsibility of royal life. You almost convinced me, until I found out what you'd done for your mother and sister after your father walked out." He looked thoughtful. "I should have guessed what was happening. Our legends say that if you survive an encounter with the serpent, he will deliver you to your true love."

She rested her head against his shoulder. "Do you believe in the legend?"

He caressed her hair before answering. "How can I not? I also started falling in love with you the day I snatched you from the serpent's jaws. Why do you think I bonded you to me?''

She lifted her head. "Because I slapped your face?''

He smiled. "I am not as fragile as all that. It was to keep you here long enough to fall in love with me.''

Confession time. "It worked, but I thought only on my side.''

"Now you know the truth. I was the one who became bonded to you, for life. I love you, *ma amouvere*. Come, let me show you around the palace, since it is to be your new home.''

"Can we start with the bedrooms first?'' she asked boldly.

He pretended shock. "What are you suggesting?''

"Well, we need to make sure the palace has enough bedrooms for all the brothers and sisters Nori is going to have after we're married,'' she promised, then paled as she remembered his reluctance to have other children around. "If you want more children, I mean,'' she said on a knife-edge of tension.

Relief flooded through her when he nodded. "It was only my thinking that I would never have them that made it so painful to be around them,'' he confessed.

Excitement curled through her, and she couldn't resist asking, "What did you think I meant when I asked you to show me the bedrooms?''

His laugh was wickedly provocative. "Perhaps, *ma amouvere, ta'amo ta'vera?*''

Without warning he swung her into his arms and she squealed a protest. "Put me down, Lorne. I was only joking. We can't go to bed for a week.''

He set her down with a show of reluctance. "You're a hard woman, Allie. And you make me a hard man.'' Pressed against him she was left in no doubt of it.

Desire tore through her, but she managed to smile around the lump clogging her throat. "I aim to please."

With a groan of surrender he molded her against him, his kisses and caresses showing her how well she had succeeded in her aim.

Epilogue

With an escort of motorcycle police, a limousine slid to a stop outside the Teresa Denys Memorial Hospital, and His Highness Prince Michel bounded out. At the main entrance he almost collided with his sister, Princess Adrienne.

She took in his casual attire at a glance. "Golf?"

He gave a rueful grin. "Marine biology. The first day in months I've been able to indulge my hobby, and our sister-in-law chooses it to go into labor. To make matters worse the helicopter was being serviced when I got your call. Are we in time?"

"Depends on whose genes win out," she said. "I don't know about Allie's side of the family, but the de Marigny offspring tend to arrive in a hurry."

Michel took her arm and escorted her into the hospital. "You sure did."

She grinned. "According to Lorne, so did you."

They were greeted by the head of the hospital who invited the royal pair to follow him to a private waiting room reserved for them in the maternity wing. When had his raven-haired little sister turned into such a beauty, Michel wondered, seeing heads turn as Adrienne passed. He was under no illusions that the admiring looks they were getting were for him. "When will we get to visit you in here?" he asked her quietly.

"When I'm as much in love as Lorne and Allie," she admitted after a long pause.

"I knew big brother was in over his head the day he brought her to Isle des Anges," Michel said. Like Adrienne, he refused offers of coffee and refreshments, feeling too keyed up to eat. If he felt so edgy, what was Lorne going through right now?

He soon found out when the door burst open and his brother charged through. One look at the grin on Lorne's face told Michel that everything was just dandy. "The staff told me you'd arrived. Just in time to greet your new niece, Aimee."

"You're naming her after her grandmother," Adrienne said with a nostalgic smile. She hugged Lorne. "How are Allie and the baby?"

"Come and see for yourself."

Allie's private room was awash with the native Carramer orchids that were her favorite flower. Lorne had built her a conservatory so she could grow them herself, Michel recalled. She was pretty good at growing things, judging from the bundle cradled in her right arm. Lorne occupied her other arm. Apart from the exhaustion they were entitled to, they looked as happy as a family could possibly look, Michel thought with a rush of affection for them.

He hesitated, fearful of intruding, but Allie's tired smile beckoned the visitors closer. "Princess Aimee, meet your uncle Michel and your aunt Adrienne."

"She's gorgeous," Adrienne said on a sigh. "You did well, Allie. Congratulations to both of you. Has Nori seen Aimee yet?"

Allie shook her head. "Laura Myss is collecting him from school and bringing him straight here. He's tickled pink about having a new baby sister, although we had to talk him out of naming her Pegasus, after his horse."

Michel tweaked the blanket down a little to get a proper look at the new arrival. With her crown of dark hair and long, dark lashes, she took his breath away. "She's going to be a beauty," he said admiringly.

Lorne caressed his wife's hair. "Just like her mother."

Adrienne perched herself on the end of the bed. "Speaking of mothers, when is yours due to arrive, Allie?"

Allie glanced at the huge basket of baby things her family had sent. "She and my stepfather are flying in later today. Lorne called them earlier, and they can't wait to meet Aimee. My mother says she still can't believe that she is grandmother to an heir to the throne of Carramer."

Allie sounded as if she had a little trouble believing it herself, Michel thought. Even after two years of marriage she still looked at Lorne as if he was a miracle she had never expected to receive. Lorne felt the same way, he had confessed to Michel, who felt a twinge of something that might or might not have been jealousy.

"When are you two going to do your bit for the succession?" demanded a crusty voice from the doorway.

They turned as one to greet Alain Pascale who wore a scrub gown with a mask hanging around his neck. "Don't look so surprised to see me. As long as I'm still breathing, I'll be helping to deliver de Marigny babies." The doctor wagged an accusing finger at Michel. "You still haven't answered my question."

Without ceremony, he took the baby from Allie and placed her in Michel's arms. The feel of the tiny, warm body melted something inside Michel, who adjusted his position to accommodate her as if he'd been doing it for years. Where did the instinct come from, he thought, gazing in wonder at the dark eyes watching him from under their fringe of long lashes.

"You're talking to a confirmed bachelor," he said with a laugh that didn't quite ring true.

Lorne laughed and shook his head. "That's what I said until Allie came along. All it takes is the right woman to change your mind."

Adrienne nodded. "I'll bet someone is waiting in the wings for you right now."

Holding the new baby carefully, afraid he might break her, Michel was inclined to dismiss his siblings' predictions as romantic fantasy. They couldn't possibly be right, could they?

The baby's angelic expression was no help except to affirm the happiness that Lorne and Allie had found with each other. Was such happiness in store for Michel himself? He could only wait…and wonder.

* * * * *

*The wait is over when Michel de Marigny
learns of a secret betrothal.
Don't miss THE PRINCE'S BRIDE-TO-BE,
the second dramatic instalment of*
THE CARRAMER CROWN,
on sale August 2000 in Silhouette Romance.

Intimate Moments is celebrating Silhouette's 20th Anniversary with groundbreaking new promotions and star authors:

Look for these original novels from
New York Times bestselling authors:

In August 2000:
A Game of Chance by **Linda Howard**, #1021

In September 2000:
Night Shield by **Nora Roberts**,
part of NIGHT TALES

Don't miss
A YEAR OF LOVING DANGEROUSLY,
a twelve-book continuity series featuring SPEAR—a
covert intelligence agency. For its equally enigmatic
operatives, love was never part of the mission profile....
Sharon Sala launches the promotion in July 2000
with *Mission: Irresistible*, #1016.

In September 2000, look for the return
of **36 HOURS**, with original stories from
**Susan Mallery, Margaret Watson,
Doreen Roberts** and **Marilyn Pappano**.

And look for:
Who Do You Love?
October 2000, #1033
You won't want to miss this two-in-one collection
featuring **Maggie Shayne** and **Marilyn Pappano**!

Available at your favorite retail outlet.

Silhouette®
Where love comes alive™

If you enjoyed what you just read,
then we've got an offer you can't resist!

Take 2 bestselling love stories FREE!

Plus get a FREE surprise gift!

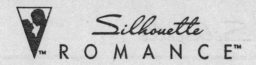

COMING NEXT MONTH

#1462 THOSE MATCHMAKING BABIES—Marie Ferrarella
Storkville, USA

With the opening of her new day-care center, Hannah Brady was swamped. Then twin babies appeared at the back door! Luckily Dr. Jackson Caldwell was *very* willing to help. In fact, Hannah soon wondered if his interest wasn't more than neighborly....

#1463 CHERISH THE BOSS—Judy Christenberry
The Circle K Sisters

Abby Kennedy was not what Logan Crawford had expected in his new boss. The Circle K's feisty owner was young, intelligent...and beautiful. And though Abby knew a lot about ranching, Logan was hoping *he* could teach *her* a few things—about love!

#1464 FIRST TIME, FOREVER—Cara Colter
Virgin Brides

She was caring for her orphaned nephew. He had a farm to run and a toddler to raise. So Kathleen Miles and Evan Atkins decided on a practical, mutually beneficial union...until the handsome groom decided to claim his virgin bride....

#1465 THE PRINCE'S BRIDE-TO-BE—Valerie Parv
The Carramer Crown

As a favor to her twin sister, Caroline Temple agreed to pose as handsome Prince Michel de Marigny's betrothed. But soon she wanted to be the prince's real-life bride. Yet if he knew the truth, would Michel accept *Caroline* as his wife?

#1466 IN WANT OF A WIFE—Arlene James

Millionaire Channing Hawkins didn't want romance, but he needed a mommy for his daughter. Lovely Jolie Winters was a perfect maternal fit, but Channing soon realized he'd gotten more than he'd wished for...and that love might be part of the package....

#1467 HIS, HERS...OURS?—Natalie Patrick

Her boss was getting married, and perfectionist Shelley Harriman wanted everything flawless. But Wayne Perry, her boss's friend, had entirely different ideas. Could these two get through planning the wedding...and admit there might be another in *their* future?